# BIRTHDAY

## KOJI SUZUKI

*Translation*
**Glynne Walley**

**ǁVERTICAL.**

Published by Vertical, an imprint of Kodansha USA Publishing, LLC.

Originally published in Japan as *Baasudei* by KADOKAWA CORPORATIC
Tokyo, 1999.

ISBN 978-1-932234-82-4

Printed in the United States of America

First Paperback Edition

Fourth Printing

Kodansha USA Publishing, LLC
451 Park Ave. South 7th Floor
New York, NY 10016
www.kodansha.us

# CONTENTS

## Coffin in the Sky
p.5

## Lemon Heart
p.47

## Happy Birthday
p.149

# COFFIN IN THE SKY

# 1

*November 1990*

Even before she'd regained consciousness, her retinas were registering the scene above her. Not that there was much to be seen: her field of vision was terribly restricted, as if she were lying in the depths of the earth gazing up at a cut-out rectangle of sky. A single vertical stripe of blue, outlined entirely in black. At first she did not know what it meant. She had no idea where she was.

The sensation was that of having just awakened, the boundary between dream and reality blurry.

Concrete walls pressed in on her from the left and the right, and she could feel the same hard substance beneath her back. Had the sky above her been round, she might have surmised that she was at the bottom of a well. But, judging from the shape, she thought it had to be a rectangular fissure several meters deep.

She couldn't see the sun directly. The clean, brisk air on her skin suggested that it was early morning. Now and then she heard crows calling with unusual presence, quite close by. They didn't show themselves, and she heard no wing beats, just their cries echoing in the narrow space.

The crows' calls abruptly ceased; in their place the sound of a ship's horn reached her ears. She was near the ocean. The faint tang of seawater tickled her nostrils. She gradually began to grasp where she was: on the roof of a building at the edge of Tokyo Bay.

Thrusting up her chin, she saw a pair of rusty pipes crossing overhead. The walls on either hand were close—too close for her to be able to move her shoulders or arms. Iron rebar poked like thorns out of the cracked concrete. It looked painful to the touch and made the space seem even more constricted. All she could do was just lie there stiff as a rod, face up, arms and legs straight.

She raised her head to try and cast a glance towards where her feet lay. Perhaps her eyes had deceived her, but she thought she'd seen something flutter in the breeze that at first she'd taken for a thin iron bar. When she focused her eyes she realized that it wasn't an iron bar at all, but a thin strip of cloth, like the sash from a bathrobe. One end was tied to something, she didn't know what, and the other end danced lazily by her feet.

...*The spider's thread.*

She recalled a short story by that title, by Ryuno-suke Akutagawa. Hell came to mind, and every pore in her body seemed to clench.

She could not recall why she'd come to such a place. Her memories were fragmentary, scattered, like broken and discarded tiles. She tried to remember, but the bits and pieces refused to form any meaningful pattern, and she couldn't distinguish cause and effect.

*Where am I? Why am I here?*

Clearly there were gaps in her memory, but she had no idea how much blank time they added up to.

She tried uttering her name, deep inside her breast. *Mai Takano.*

That was probably correct. She was fairly certain that she was, in fact, a woman named Mai Takano. Yet, it somehow didn't feel right. She had the inescapable feeling that some strange entity had entered her body— she felt like she wasn't herself. She'd felt like that for a while now.

She tried to recall her age, her address, the chronology of her life, any information she could come up with that might sharpen the outlines of who she was.

*I'm 22. I'm a college student. I'm a liberal arts major, and I'm hoping to go on to grad school to study philosophy.*

Suddenly her legs hurt. Or, rather, for the first time since she'd awakened, she registered the fact that her ankles were giving her pain.

Mai Takano raised her head apprehensively and looked toward her feet. A shock greeted her: she couldn't see them.

Some object was obstructing her vision, something she couldn't identify. She squinted at it. Finally, her eyes grew wide and her expression became one of astonishment as she realized that it was her own swollen belly.

She had tucked her sweatshirt into her jumper skirt, but now her midriff under the skirt was swollen tight as a drum. Forgetting the pain in her legs, Mai placed one hand gingerly on her abdomen. She no longer felt as if a foreign object had lodged itself within her belly. Now she could feel that her belly and the hand that was touching it were contiguous, part of the same flesh. The swelling came from within her body, stretching taut the skin of her abdomen. As far as she could remember, she was a thin girl—breasts not at all on the large side, waist size proudly smaller than average.

She was not afraid. Nor did she despair. After her initial astonishment passed, she just lay there in a daze for a while running her hands over her abdomen. She couldn't believe she'd been placed in such a situation. She didn't know what to feel.

A cool, objective gaze examined her body. Her mind was a blank, as though her intellect had ceased to function. She scrutinized her swollen belly with the gaze of another; no matter how she looked at it, she was a woman about to give birth. The word "pregnant" came to mind.

That was the catalyst. Fragmented images revived one after another in Mai's mind. Her intuition told her why she was where she was. It had begun with—yes, a videotape.

*It's because I watched it.*

She'd had a bad feeling about it, but she'd watched it anyway. And she shouldn't have.

Mai remembered inserting the tape into the video deck, the touch of her finger on the play button—it all came back to her now. It all felt real.

# 2

It was a simple chain of events, really, that brought the tape into her hands and that led her to watch it. Mai had no way of knowing whether a will operated behind the veneer of chance. Perhaps, too afraid of a power that couldn't be seen, she bullied herself into believing that it was all mere coincidence. Maybe she wanted *not* to know the truth.

Ryuji Takayama's friend Asakawa had told her, in so many words, that a videotape had been involved in his demise. No one bothered to tell her exactly what the connection might be. Perhaps Ryuji watched something so strange, he died of shock—that was the preposterous theory of Mai's concoction. But how else could a videotape cause a man's death? What other explanation could there possibly be?

And otherwise, Asakawa's question made no sense. He'd asked Mai, since she'd been in contact with Ryuji in his final moments, "He didn't tell you anything there at the end? No last words? Nothing, say, about a videotape?"

He'd made it sound like some videotape had brought about Ryuji's death.

Mai didn't believe it, in the end. And that was why

she allowed herself to be led—quite easily at that—into watching it herself.

Ryuji had taught logic at the university. He'd been writing a philosophical treatise and serializing it in a monthly journal. Mai, a student of his, was in charge of making a clean copy of each month's installment for submission; Ryuji's handwriting was all but illegible to anybody who hadn't spent time getting used to it. Mai had volunteered for the job not out of slavish sacrifice but because the task would secure her the honor of being her mentor's first reader.

Ryuji had just finished the final installment when he'd suddenly departed this life. According to Mitsuo Ando, the coroner who performed Ryuji's autopsy, he'd died from sudden myocardial infarction due to a blockage in the coronary artery. But questions remained, and then there was what Asakawa had said. He was Ryuji's friend, and he'd implied that a videotape he'd watched had caused his death. The circumstances of Ryuji's death got murkier and murkier.

Mai, meanwhile, was due to hand in Ryuji's final installment to his editor when she discovered that there were pages missing from the manuscript. This was the conclusion, the wrap-up to a year-long project, and there were pages missing.

She went over his apartment with a fine-toothed comb, with no luck. Her last hope was Ryuji's parents' home in Sagami Ohno. Immediately after his death, everything in his apartment had been packed up and sent

12

back there; it was the only place she could imagine the missing pages being.

So Mai explained the situation to Ryuji's mother and got permission to visit. Mai was shown to the second floor of the house and to the room that Ryuji had used as a study from elementary school through his sophomore year in college. Ryuji's mother told Mai she could search the room to her heart's content.

Books, clothing, appliances, small pieces of furniture: everything Ryuji had had in his one-bedroom apartment was there, stuffed into the cardboard boxes stacked randomly around the room. Mai was looking for a few pieces of paper—they could be anywhere. Foreseeing a lengthy slog, Mai took off her cardigan and set to work.

After a while the search began to seem a pointless one for the proverbial needle in a haystack. But she couldn't think of any other way to plug the gap in the manuscript. She'd just have to keep looking.

But as her will weakened so did her body. Fatigue came into her hunched shoulders. Now and then she thought she could feel someone's gaze fixed on her back, and the sense that she was being watched only grew stronger as the minutes went by.

In high school, she had modeled—just once—for an oil painting by her homeroom teacher, an art instructor. Needless to say she'd been fully clothed, but all the same she'd had the impression that the teacher's gaze had passed right through her clothing to lap at her skin, indeed to penetrate right to her skeletal structure. She'd known a curious arousal, half embarrassment and half rapture. Later she'd heard that when painting a person's head, the artist's eyes are really seeing the skull. Her intuition hadn't been far off and she'd thought, *That stare of his saw straight to my pelvic bone.*

That same powerful, razor gaze was boring into her back, penetrating her skin, gouging away her flesh, trying to feel her bones.

Mai couldn't bear it any longer. She turned around. Behind her she saw a black object, half covered by the pink cardigan she'd taken off prior to beginning her search. She'd placed her cardigan on the object without noticing it.

She moved the garment to reveal a black-bodied VCR. The unit wasn't turned on, but its pilot light glowed a dull red. Mai remembered what Asakawa had said to her.

*He didn't tell you anything there at the end? No last words? Nothing, say, about a videotape?*

Those words urged her to it. She turned on the video deck.

# 3

She began to think, gradually with greater certainty, that she was there because she was supposed to be there. It was no accident, but a necessary thing.

Now that she thought about it, the shape of the rooftop fissure where she was resembled a videocassette. A long, narrow rectangle. No, that wasn't quite it. It was more accurate to say that it was shaped like the *case* of a videocassette.

She wasn't sure what the purpose of the hole was in terms of the building's design. An exhaust shaft, maybe a drainage shaft? Skyscraper construction was a field she knew nothing about. She could hear the whine of a motor beneath the concrete, which suggested the building had an elevator. She was somewhere near the machine room, then. She knew that much.

The sky suddenly brightened, going from a whitish to a truer blue. A line that divided light from shadow was crossing the shaft wall fast enough that she could actually see it advancing downward. Light was moving into the giant videocassette case.

Mai recalled the moment at Ryuji's parents' house when she'd taken the tape from the VCR. She'd plugged in the machine, turned it on, and pressed eject. A *kachunk*, and the tape popped out like a child sticking its tongue out at her.

She remembered the touch of it, hard, inorganic but strangely warm. She'd only just turned on the power, but it communicated to her fingers an almost living heat.

A title was written on the spine. *Liza Minnelli, Frank Sinatra, Sammy Davis, Jr./1989.*

The handwriting wasn't very good, and she didn't think the inscription described the contents of the tape. She doubted it actually contained a concert. Most likely someone had recorded something else over it, but left the title.

What she regretted most now, more than watching the tape, was sneaking it out of Ryuji's parents' house and taking it home with her. Why couldn't she just leave it alone? She'd gone there to find those missing pages. She should have ignored the odd tape. The moment she took it home with her, her fate was sealed: sooner or later, she'd watch it.

The line descended along the wall of the shaft in leaps. Suddenly, the light hit her straight in the eyes. The sun was directly overhead now.

Time was flying; it was not passing in an analog manner. She'd awakened only just now, in the early morning, but the sunlight had reached the bottom of the hole. It had to be noon or thereabouts.

She lifted her left arm, weakly. No wristwatch. She'd have to tell time by the position of the sun.

She was probably still losing memory—a block at a

time. That would explain the jerky, disjointed passage of time. She was alternating between awareness and blank-outs. She'd spent the hours since her first awakening in a state of idleness, drifting in a daze or lost in flashbacks.

But now she knew exactly what she had to do.

*I need to figure out how to get out of here.*

She'd die if she didn't escape—and death would come slowly, at its leisure, nibbling away at her soul.

*Have I already gone crazy?*

She knew, considering her predicament, that she should be terrified, perhaps even in a state of panic, yet she was calm. It was as if there was another her some-where watching it all as a bystander. She wondered if she was capable of fully appreciating her situation given the gaps in her awareness, the tenuousness of her hold on consciousness.

For no apparent reason, Mai found herself thinking of a pretty girl rotting at the bottom of a well. The image had to have been triggered by something, but what? The smell? She was aware of a citrusy scent wafting on the air that seemed to stimulate her imagination. The image of the girl became more and more real; it leaned heavily on Mai's body, and then drew back.

Mai had imagined a girl as if she were really there.

She listened closely and tuned herself to her sur-roundings. It was terrifying, this being utterly alone, and she wanted someone—anyone—to come to her.

Her ears were all she could rely on, and she waited desperately for the sound of footsteps. She was vexed at her own powerlessness.

*So I have to wait to be rescued?* She'd never liked to be so passive about anything.

The thread dangling down into the shaft was her lifeline, her only connection with the bustling world below. She wondered how many bathrobe sashes had been tied together to make it. Looking up at it, she could only see one knot. What was it doing there anyway? If the sash was a snake, the knot would be its head.

It looked too slender to hold her weight, but it was the only way out she could see. The end of the sash-rope swung lazily in the air a foot above the floor.

She decided to try to force herself into a sitting position to see how much she could move. As she made the attempt, she banged her injured left ankle into the wall and nearly screamed from the pain. Was it broken or just sprained? The intense pain proved to her, at any rate, that she was indeed conscious, and it ended up giving her a little courage.

She broke into a cold sweat as she tried to steel herself against the pain. But how could she expect to climb out on her own if she couldn't even sit up?

*Call for help.*

Mai racked her brain for a way to let the inhabitants of the outside world know she was there.

She cried out, just to see how it went. "Help! Help me!" The sky above swallowed her words. She seriously doubted anybody could have heard her. Unless somebody came up onto the roof, yelling wasn't going to do her any good.

She pondered. If nobody was going to come up to the roof on their own initiative, she'd have to do something to draw attention to herself, to bring somebody up.

Maybe passersby would look up if something came falling out of the sky.

*Is there anything I can throw?*

She stretched out her arms and felt around above her head until she found a few chunks of concrete. She picked one up and examined it. It was about the size of her thumb. It was just a little piece of old concrete from the crumbling wall; even if it happened to hit somebody in the head it probably wouldn't cause serious injury.

Mai had been on the track team in middle school and high school, as a sprinter, and she had confidence in her athletic ability. She'd been able to throw a softball farther than almost anybody in her class. But she'd never tried throwing from her current position before—flat on her back. The only feasible motion was to swing her right arm in an arc from her head toward her feet; it meant there was only one direction in which she could toss the concrete. If she couldn't get it over the railing at the edge of the rooftop, the whole thing would be a waste of effort.

The sun was descending into the west. She realized that if she was going to try this, she should do it in daylight when there would be a maximum number of people walking by. She flung the piece of concrete into the air. It immediately disappeared from sight, swallowed up soundlessly by the sky.

She was astonished how little of the world she could see. Her entire world was that narrow strip of sky. The ease with which the concrete had disappeared made her wonder if the place she was in really connected to the world below.

She felt around again and this time found a four-inch length of iron pipe. Big enough and heavy enough, she thought, to carry farther than the fragment of concrete. On the other hand, if it hit someone in the head it could do considerable damage.

She wanted to minimize the pipe's potential to do injury. She also wanted to lend it some trace of herself, to make it seem like a message.

She fished in her pockets for a scrap of cloth. A handkerchief would do—anything, really. If she could tie something to the pipe, then whoever found it would be less likely to think it had simply fallen at random.

But she had no handkerchief in her pockets. She tried to tear off a piece of her sweatshirt, a bit of the hem of her jumper, to no avail. She closed her eyes to think of her options, and an idea came to her. The odder the item attached to the pipe, the more attention it would elicit. She'd take off her panties and tie them to the pipe.

She'd have one chance. If she screwed it up, that would be it. But her only fear at the moment was that getting them off her legs might hurt too much.

She slowly hiked up her skirt and felt around in the area of her hipbone. Her skin was bare. She should have encountered the elastic band of her underwear, but all her fingernails found was her own skin. She felt all around but couldn't locate her panties.

*What the...? I'm not wearing any underwear!*

This was not normal for her. She'd never gone out in public wearing nothing under her clothes.

She raised her head and craned her neck to a painful angle in order to get a glimpse of her groin, but her distended belly was in the way. She had to judge by feel. At the very moment she realized she really wasn't wearing any underwear, her arm felt something moving inside her abdomen.

It felt precisely like a baby stirring in her womb. But then she remembered that she was still a virgin, and her consciousness threatened to recede again. Her puzzlement as to why she wasn't wearing panties gave way instantly: what was this in her womb?

She could see part of her belly now, peeking out of her rolled-up skirt. It was swollen, but it was also moving, changing shape before her eyes, in response to pressure from within.

She remembered a scene from a movie she'd seen years ago. The sheer abnormality of her situation chilled Mai to her core now.

# 4

Her memories couldn't be wrong about it. Mai knew it was foolish even to examine them.

Once, and only once, she'd nearly yielded herself physically to a boyfriend. She'd been in the same position she was in now, flat on her back, arms and legs extended. On the single bed in his apartment... They'd had long, serious discussions about it, and she was ready.

His name was Sugiyama, and he was a student at her college; both of them were in the school of liberal arts. Sugiyama was slender, pale, and handsome. A little taller than Mai, with something of the beautiful boy about him. In terms of looks, he and Mai were a fine couple.

Mai, though, wasn't attracted to his looks, but to his precociousness as a scholar. Sugiyama prided himself on knowing everything about everything, and he could answer seemingly any question with ease. It was fun just to ask him questions, so sharp was his mental razor, and conversation with him was a joy.

He was well versed in literature and was a real charmer the way he peppered conversation with bits of astrology or Greek mythology. Having devoted most of her attention to sports in high school, Mai had vowed to focus on academics in college. She fell head over heels for Sugiyama's mind—not that his androgynous good looks didn't help.

Friends who knew her as a dedicated member of the track team expressed doubts about her choice of boyfriend. *Hey, I thought you went for jocks!* That was the gist of their doubts. But Mai knew that if she had to choose between body and mind, she'd choose the latter as the locus of talent without hesitation. Of course, to have both would be ideal. But she wouldn't meet a man like that until Ryuji.

Several upperclassmen had asked her out back in high school. Although they were all pretty naïve and none of them actually tried to move on her, just sitting across the table from that type came to be a burden for Mai, what with their masculine passions and ghastly thirst for sex.

Sugiyama's androgyny comforted her, in a way. She didn't have to worry about blocking his lust, or taming it and diverting it. That was a relief and it made him relaxing to be around.

That time in his apartment when they nearly hooked up, it began almost as a sort of ritual. They proceeded with great deliberation, and only after confirming each other's feelings and intentions. At that moment, Mai had no reservations about discarding her virginity.

Following his instructions, she lay down on his bed and shut her eyes tightly. Her nervousness had made her arms and legs tense. Just as now, her limbs were straight and rigid. Sugiyama didn't try to alleviate her tension.

Rather, he went about his business in stony silence, almost seeming to enjoy the stiffness of her body.

He slowly took off her clothes and exposed her skin. Mai could see her own naked body in her mind. He simply undressed her, with no kisses or caresses, nothing to blur the roles of undresser and undressee. As pre-intercourse ceremonial, it was strangely monotonous, but Mai didn't have enough experience to think it odd.

It happened when she'd been reduced to bra and panties, and Sugiyama laid his hands on her chest. Her bra slipped upward and exposed her smallish breasts. Never very big at the best of times, they looked perfectly flat when she was supine. She imagined her breasts the way Sugiyama would be looking at them. Her nipples, large in proportion to her breasts, must have been erect and pointing at the ceiling.

The image of that moment remained vivid in Mai's memory, no doubt because it had been the product of her imagination to begin with.

She was left in that state for a dozen or more seconds, her breasts visible beneath her displaced bra. It was an awkward limbo that emphasized the flatness of her chest. She thought she could feel Sugiyama's gaze. Then the current shifted subtly—she detected a change in the air that filled her with unease.

*What are you doing? Hurry up!*

But he didn't hurry. In fact, he started to replace her bra.

At the touch of his hands on her chest, Mai's eyes

popped open. She stared in disbelief as he covered up her breasts. And not only her breasts. He put all her clothes back on her, retracing his earlier steps in reverse. He closed her away, just as innocent as she had been before, with not so much as a drop of his saliva upon her.

She looked the question into his eyes.

...*Why?*

Sugiyama leaned close and whispered into Mai's ear, "I guess we'd better not."

The blunt inadequacy of the words belied his usual eloquence. Sugiyama should have been able to come up with some pretty-sounding explanation for why he'd stopped in the middle. But he hadn't even tried. He had simply said "let's not."

Mai's mind went blank with confusion. She felt humiliated, robbed of her dignity as a person, reduced to the status of a dress-up doll.

They'd agreed to have sex. Why did he feel it necessary to do a u-turn like that? Was her body so unattractive? His refusal to explain allowed all sorts of doubts to bloom in her mind. She couldn't understand what had killed his desire. She could only despair.

*Is it because my breasts are so small?* she asked herself. But he hadn't needed to undress her to find that out. It was obvious, to a degree, even when she was clothed.

Hurt, and without finding out why, she left Sugiyama's apartment and went home.

Their relationship ended there.

She'd had boyfriends since, and they'd tried, but

she'd never crossed the line. Those dozen or so seconds of blankness always came back to haunt her. She felt like he'd evaluated her nakedness; she didn't like it. She'd rather stay a virgin for the rest of her life than go through that again.

There could be no mistake, no gap in her memory, about it. There was no point to any further scrutinizing the fact that she'd never had sex. That was a sure premise.

*So then why am I pregnant?*

Cause and effect. When something happened, there was a reason for it. The only immediate cause she could think of—yes, having watched that tape.

Then, she remembered something else, too.

*I was ovulating the day I watched it.*

She knew it, based on her cycle and on the thermometer. Her ovulation, that tape. The two had somehow come together to produce the change in her body.

The line between shadow and light was climbing the wall now. The sun was sinking, and the rectangular space was coming under the inexorable rule of darkness again.

Mai felt an appraising gaze on her body, like Sugiyama's. But there was nobody at the lip of the fissure peering in. The gaze emanated from within her own womb. The eyes she carried within were watching her.

As if to prove it, her belly undulated again with small but sharp movements.

# 5

In the end, she never was able to locate the missing pages among Ryuji's household effects. She'd promised the editor she'd have the manuscript to him by the next day. She had until the next afternoon to provide a clean copy of the final installment of the series.

It was late in the evening. Mai had locked herself in her studio apartment. She had spread the manuscript out before her on the table, and now sat there groaning, her head in her hands. It was a small room—five mats or so in size. She sat on the floor with a backrest propping her up at a low table that she used as a desk. This was how she always studied. From where she was sitting, her bookcase was close enough that she could reach out and touch it. The bookcase housed a fourteen-inch TV with a built-in VCR.

She didn't know what to do about the manuscript. Over and over she'd look up and heave a sigh. How was she going to make up for the missing section?

Mai had been concentrating on filling in the gap with her own words. There was a clear leap in logic from the previous installment to this final one. She'd been trying to supplement the argument; that was what had her stalled and groaning, her head aching.

Suddenly it occurred to her. Instead of trying to add, why not subtract? *I'm stuck because I'm trying to add words, and they won't come.* It would be much easier to pare down what was there until it made sense. She wouldn't be as liable to twist Ryuji's thoughts that way.

As soon as she'd decided on her new plan, her spirits rose. Now there looked to be a good chance of getting it done by morning.

The videotape seized that moment to catch her eye. It was what she'd found instead of the missing pages. She'd brought it back with her and placed it carelessly on top of her television. She could watch the tape now, to refresh her mind, and still have time to finish the manuscript by morning.

Thinking back now, Mai felt she had been snared, and quite cunningly. She didn't know who had set the trap, but she'd certainly been carried along by that unseen being's schemes.

From where she sat on the floor it was a natural motion for Mai to reach out and pick up the videotape.

*Liza Minnelli, Frank Sinatra, Sammy Davis, Jr./1989.*

There was no case, just the cassette.

The handwriting on the label told her that the tape didn't belong to Ryuji. Made by an unknown third party, brought into his apartment by some unknown route, it had made its way into Mai's room now to emit its strange pull.

She reached out and put the tape into the VCR. The

unit came on automatically. She switched the channel to video and pressed play.

*There's still time—throw it away!*

But the static of the tape drowned out the voice of instinct.

She couldn't fight her curiosity. The screen dissolved into a chaos to match the static. Then an image like spilled ink leapt into her vision. It was too late to turn back now. Mai steeled her nerves and sat up straight. The tape seemed to emanate arrogance, to demand close attention from whoever watched it.

*Watch until the end. You will be eaten by the lost.*

The thick stream of ink formed itself into a threat. The blinking points of light emitted an artificial brightness not possible in reality. When it pierced her eyeballs it should have been unpleasant, but she couldn't look away.

The tape was a collection of fragmentary images whose meaning was unclear. But each scene, taken on its own, had great impact, a real you-are-there quality that seemed to come straight at her. She began to wonder if the images weren't having a physical effect on her, so powerful they were.

A spray of red flashed across the screen at one point, then to change into a stream of lava that Mai saw at once was flowing down the scorched sides of a volcano. Sparks danced up into the night sky. A perfectly natural scene.

The next moment, the character for "mountain,"

*yama*, was floating in black against a white background, fading in and out of view. Then a pair of dice were tumbling around in a lead bowl.

In the following scene, a person appeared for the first time. An old woman sitting on a tatami mat, facing forward and mumbling something. It was a dialect Mai couldn't make out. The old woman seemed to be lecturing somebody, preaching.

A newborn baby gave its first cry. As Mai watched it, the baby grew larger and larger. Mai felt that she was holding the onscreen baby with her own two hands. Her palms touched skin covered in amniotic fluid. It was slick, and she felt like it slipped out of her hands. Reflexively she drew back her hands.

At the same time, the baby disappeared, and a crowd of voices erupted in cries of "Liar!" and "Fraud!" She saw a hundred faces crammed into a grid like a huge chessboard; each face wore an accusatory expression when she looked at them. The faces divided like cells until they became tiny dots filling the screen.

In the center of the black screen floated the character *sada*.

A man's face suddenly came into view. An abrupt transformation. His breathing grew ragged and huge beads of perspiration appeared on his face. Scattered trees stood behind him.

He seemed to be running—his naked shoulders gleamed with sweat. His sunburned skin was peeling. Both the background and the man's appearance were summer itself. His eyes were bloodshot, murderous. His mouth was twisted, and he was drooling; he looked upward, and then disappeared from view.

When he reappeared, a chunk of flesh had been gouged out of his shoulder, and he was bleeding profusely. Great drops of blood fell onto the screen.

The baby cried again, somewhere. A chaotic cry, it vibrated not against her eardrums but directly against her skin cells. Mai recalled the touch of the infant's flesh.

In the center of the screen there was a bright, round hole. It was like looking up in the dark at a full moon directly overhead. After a while, a rock fell from the moon, then another.

*This person's looking up from the bottom of a well.*

The moment she saw the scene, Mai grasped the situation. Maybe her intuition was at work, guessing at the fate that would later befall her.

Because, at that point, there was no reason for her to think that the moonlike circle was the lip of a well.

Finally, more words appeared. *Those who have viewed these images are fated to die at this exact hour one week from now. If you do not wish to die, you must follow these instructions exactly...*

And then the scene changed. The concatenation of images was replaced by a commercial for mosquito-repelling coils that she'd seen on TV numerous times. A commercial had been taped over the instructions for avoiding death. They had been erased.

With a trembling hand Mai pushed the stop button.

Her jaw was shaking; she was trying to speak, but the words wouldn't come. But she was alone—who was she trying to talk to?

The existence of a videotape that killed its viewers in a week's time...

When Asakawa had asked her about Ryuji's death, he'd said, *He didn't tell you anything there at the end? No last words? Nothing, say, about a videotape?*

The tape had been in Ryuji's room. Ryuji had watched it, and a week later he'd died mysteriously.

If she hadn't watched the tape herself, she'd never buy such a scenario. But she had watched it. Every scene had exuded a reality that she could feel in her very cells.

Something was rising within her. She'd been sitting, stunned, in front of the VCR, but now she felt like she had to throw up. She dashed into the bathroom.

*I shouldn't have watched it.*

It was too late for regrets. Besides, she hadn't so much watched it of her own free will as been forced to watch it, by the will of another, she felt.

Mai stuck her finger down her throat and vomited until her stomach was empty. At that moment she wanted to rid herself of everything that was inside her. She felt like some foreign object had gotten into her.

Choking on bile, she began to weep. She knelt in front of the toilet, weakened, gasping for breath.

For a time, she could feel herself slowly vanishing—and then she passed out.

Since watching the tape, Mai suffered frequent lapses in her consciousness. She was unable to recall the events of the preceding week in order and complete. She'd suddenly realize that several hours had passed and not know where she was. It was as if something had possessed her soul.

...*As if something had possessed my soul.*

That was definitely the phrase for it. She was dimly aware that her body was being controlled.

The foreign object that had entered her during her viewing of the tape gradually grew. Perhaps her watching it while ovulating had facilitated the thing's invasion of her. Or maybe it happened to everyone who watched the video—maybe it was how they went down the road to death.

Mai pictured countless sperm charging toward the egg in her oviduct. Once, in a sex-ed textbook, she'd seen a very graphic representation of it. Viral microorganisms, generating and proliferating within her from watching that tape, overwhelming her oviduct—if that wasn't it, then she had no idea how she'd ended up a virgin with the body of a pregnant woman.

There was life within her belly, that was for sure. It pulsed, and it waved its arms and legs inside her tightly-stretched womb.

# 6

The end of the rope tickled her somewhere in the vicinity of her bended knees. It seemed to hang lower than it had the last time she'd looked, at midday.

*Who hung that rope there, and why?*

But she hardly needed to pose the question. The sensation of tying one end of the sash to the railing on the rooftop revived in Mai's hands. Images were being inserted into her consciousness, like flash photos, and she could see herself from a bystander's perspective in the darkness. That was Mai herself tying the knot with impatient finger, overriden by a will not her own. Her legs and waist were shaky and were ready to give out at any moment, yet, driven by an unfathomable sense of duty, she was focused on tying the makeshift rope.

The rope was all ready at the time she left her apartment. There was one other item she'd prepared along with it, but the memory was missing. She wondered what it was. Something in a plastic bag, she knew. She could recall the feel of something squishy.

The life that had started growing within her after viewing the tape had, at some point, begun to exert its influence over her body. Sometimes, in the middle of the night, she would abruptly come to, and listening she'd hear the pulse of whatever it was in her belly. It only took four or five days for her abdomen to swell to the point that she seemed ready to deliver, and the same time for her enlarged nipples to start leaking milk.

Why was she there at the bottom of the crack in the top of a building? All at once, Mai knew.

*To give birth.*

She didn't believe for a moment that the thing within her was her own child. She wasn't even sure it was human.

*A beast.*

No—she didn't even feel it was a life form.

But she felt a sense of responsibility; she had to birth this unknown thing without anybody knowing. She didn't know where the sense came from, but come it did, and there was no resisting it. It drove her to act, to fulfill her role as a cocoon.

At around the same hour the day before, Mai had taken off her underwear, snuck out of her apartment, and ascended to the roof of this building in the warehouse district, where few people walked at night and few cars passed. A dilapidated old building by the Shore Road.

She had climbed over the gate on the second floor landing and climbed the spiraling fire escape to the top of the building. Once there, she'd climbed by ladder to the rooftop and gone over to the machine room. On the seaward side of it there was a deep exhaust shaft, like a coffin floating in the sky.

A perfect place for the pupa to escape its cocoon. A

35

perfect place for the soul to discard its shell. It wasn't far from Mai's apartment, and it was almost guaranteed that no one would see.

Mai had tried to climb down into the shaft using the sash-rope. She'd fallen and sprained her ankle.

*What time is it, I wonder.*

During the day she'd been able to guess the time based on the shifting sunlight, but it was several hours past sundown now. Stars shone, but they didn't help her. She had no way to gauge the passage of time.

Twenty-four hours, perhaps, had gone by since she left her apartment.

Suddenly sadness overcame Mai. She'd been there for twenty-four hours, but for most of that time her consciousness had been elsewhere; she'd only been herself for two or three hours at the most. During those hours, she had known astonishment, and fear, and unutterable dread, but this was the first time she'd felt sadness.

Her body no doubt knew that her time was approaching.

She tried to get up but couldn't; she tried to cry out but found her throat as though blocked. Meanwhile, the movements within her womb grew more violent as the power pressing on her from inside overflowed with life.

Her vitality was being transferred out of her. She reflected on her twenty-two years with chagrin. Had she lived merely to have her body taken over, to give birth to this unknown thing? How pitiful.

Mai knew the meaning of her own tears. Fear of the

thing that was trying to nullify her life was also forcing her grief to the surface.

It was mid-November. They'd had bright, clear weather for several days now, but it was cold in the middle of the night. The chill of the concrete seeped through her back and into her bones, only adding to her sorrow. And now a thin film of water coated the inner surfaces of the walls. A leak from somewhere? The clamminess made things still worse.

She was sobbing now.

*Help! Help me!*

She couldn't voice the words. Then the labor pains started, and they washed away her sadness and the cold, along with every other feeling and sensation, on a mammoth ocean wave. The smell of the sea was stronger now. It had to be high tide.

She remembered something her mother had told her once, when she was little.

*You were born at high tide.*

Her mother believed that if the rhythm of nature wasn't disrupted, people were born at high tide and died at low tide.

But Mai had the encroaching feeling that life and death were going to be simultaneous. Did that mean it was high tide or low tide now? Shifts in gravity, either way, influenced life and death.

The contractions subsided a bit; the rhythm of the waves slowed. She thought she could hear a melody, low over the rhythm. The horns of ships and distant cars provided effective accents. Was it just the city's night sounds coming together in all their layers to sound like music, or was there actually a melody playing somewhere in the building? Or still...

Mai couldn't decide if she was really hearing music. She wouldn't be able to distinguish a real sound from an auditory hallucination. All she knew was that listening to it calmed her down.

The mysterious melody softened her pain and put her into a peculiar mood. Suddenly, she knew where the music was coming from. But, no, it couldn't be. She tried to suppress her own realization, raising her head and staring at her belly.

*Who's that singing—down there...*

She imagined the life inside her singing to ease its mother's pain. Her dark womb, filled with amniotic fluid—didn't it bear a resemblance to the space Mai was in? And the thing singing softly in that dark place was about to show its face.

The voice was that of a young female. At moments it seemed to be coming from right next to Mai's ears, at others to wend its way up to her from below her feet. Finally, the voice stopped singing and began speaking, low and soft.

The words were those of a woman who had died, once. She said so.

*I died at the bottom of a well, you know.*

The woman gave her name as Sadako Yamamura. She proceeded to describe her past in brief.

Mai was unable to disbelieve. The voice said that

the images on the videotape had not been recorded by any camera. Rather, they'd been experienced by Sadako's five senses and then projected by the operation of her thoughts. It made sense to Mai and she accepted it; when she had watched the images on the tape, her perceptions had been completely fused with those of this unknown woman Sadako. The image of the baby, incredibly vivid, flashed across Mai's mind.

Her cervix was fully dilated. All alone, Mai heaved, in rhythm with her contractions. Her tortured moans echoed in the narrow space, she could hear them. But it didn't sound like her own voice and she felt strange.

The labor pains were coming closer together than at first, and as the interval shortened, energy concentrated and released itself more intensely towards birth, uterus and muscle contracting again and again.

Giant waves crashed one after another in Mai's brain. In time with them she sucked in a lungful of air, pushed, and bit back the scream that wanted to come out as she focused all her strength on her lower body.

High tide must have been approaching, the moon rounding the earth.

A sudden violent contraction came over Mai. Energy concentrated in her lower abdomen and was poised to shoot through the exit as a lump. Mai stretched out her arms, reaching for something, anything, to cling to.

*It's coming!*

When the intuition coursed through her, consciousness receded.

# 7

She had probably only been out for a few minutes. As consciousness returned, Mai's retinas registered the small shadow wiggling between her thighs.

The baby crawled out of her womb without a cry. It twisted and turned, trying to sit up. It was using its hands skillfully, like a swimmer. Its movements, all the more because they weren't accompanied by cries, asserted that it already had a will of its own.

Mai found herself completely devoid of the joy and awe that motherhood was supposed to bring. The thing was finally born—that fact alone gradually spread across her body. Relief at having expelled the foreign object won out over all other emotion.

As her eyes adjusted, she could see the little form more clearly.

Covered with amniotic fluid, its skin glistening in the starlight, the baby was grabbing furiously at some rope-like thing with both hands. A wrinkly rope, extending from Mai's body... The baby had in its grasp the umbilical cord.

The thing had been born, but it was not yet fully separate from Mai's body. The umbilical cord still connected them. Just as the sash-rope still hung down into the rooftop crevice. Mai wanted to sever the cord and be done with it. Yet, powerless, she was forced to just lie there and let happen what might.

The baby was as active as Mai was enervated. It stretched out the ropy umbilical cord with its hands and then placed it in its mouth. It was trying to sever the cord. Naturally, its teeth hadn't come in yet; the way it clamped the cord between its red gums and shook its head from side to side, the thing was a far cry from an infant: its little face was demonic.

In the end, the process was like ripping apart sausage links. Having cut the cord, the baby took a wet towel from the plastic bag lying at Mai's feet and started to wipe off its body.

Mai herself must have prepared the wet towel at the same time she'd made the sash-rope. The bag had probably landed at her feet when she'd fallen into the hole. She hadn't seen it from the way her head lay.

She'd been preparing to give birth without realizing it. She must have been taking commands from the embryo growing in her womb. Not that that made any sense.

Mai's uterus continued to contract. She pushed a little more, and thought she could feel the placenta coming out. Once the placenta and fetal membranes had been expelled, her belly was flat again.

Now that she could see over herself, she had a much clearer view of the baby.

It was wiping off its body, slowly, as if trying to get

the wrinkles out of its skin. It had known in the womb what it had to do once it got out. It moved with alarming dexterity.

After it had finished wiping itself off, the baby assumed a relaxed, crouching pose and started moving its mouth.

*What's it doing?*

From the way it moved its face and hands, it looked to be eating something. Its ravenous expression stimulated Mai's own appetite, and she raised her head.

Dark, discolored blood clung to its tiny lips. She could hear it chewing flesh.

It was eating the placenta.

Stuffing its cheeks with the placenta—no doubt extremely nutritious—the baby seemed to surge with vitality. As it ate this piece of Mai, who herself was hungry and weak, it wore a satisfied smile.

Their eyes met in the darkness. For a moment, the little face took on an expression of pity.

Mai managed to speak.

"Are you Sadako Yamamura?"

The baby's gaze was steady as it bowed a head plastered with downy hair. The thing was apparently affirming that it was Sadako.

The sash-rope dangled just above the baby, caressing its shoulder.

Like one determined, the baby grabbed the end of the rope. Then it stood there like that for a while, staring at Mai. Mai could tell that it meant to go up into the world outside—to climb up the rope and to make its escape.

Just as she'd thought, the baby started to pull itself up the rope. Partway up, however, it stopped and looked down at Mai. It blinked and gave her a meaningful look. Was it trying to tell her something? Its face was expressionless—she saw no hostility there, no sympathy, no hatred, nothing, perhaps because it wasn't possible to read any kind of expression into such a tiny, wrinkled face.

Finally it reached the rim of the exhaust shaft. It stood there, silhouetted against the stars. Mai could see the outline of its poorly severed umbilical cord—it looked like the tail of an animal or the horn of a demon.

The baby stood there at the rim for a while, looking down at her. Mai found herself clinging to that black shape.

*Help me.*

There was no one else around. The only one she could turn to for help was this being she'd given birth to. She would normally be caring for it, but their positions were reversed.

But her wish was in vain. The baby began to pull the rope up just as it had forcibly shredded the umbilical cord. If it allowed the connection to remain, perhaps it couldn't truly stand on its own.

Mai understood, but she wished it would just leave the rope, at least. Why did it have to take away her only conduit to the outside world? *Don't cut the spider's thread, I'll never be able to crawl up out of hell!*

Mai begged, implored; she hated the baby's cruelty.

But its movements were calm and measured. Perhaps it, too, was acting under the compulsion of some tragic sense of duty. It gave no indication, in any case, that it would heed Mai's request.

*I beg of you, don't abandon me.*

The rope finished its ascent, and the baby's face disappeared from the rim of the exhaust shaft. What was it doing now? Mai could hear it doing something; it hadn't left yet.

The baby peeked back over the edge again, and then, with a quick movement of its left arm, tossed something down to Mai. Against the dim sky it looked like a snake twisted in a spiral. It was the sash-rope, all coiled up. It landed weightlessly on Mai's midsection and lay there in rings. Just a prank? Mai could detect no meaning in it, only the stench of malice.

The baby flashed her a grin. Then, without a trace of reluctance, it disappeared into the night.

Where was it going and what did it desire to become?

Mai kept seeing the umbilical cord hanging from its belly. The image resonated with her and would not leave. It reminded her of a demon—no image fit it better.

She heard the horn of a ship on Tokyo Bay. The sound was like a wolf's howl, a creature's vivid wail. In response came the faint yapping of a dog from somewhere in the residential neighborhood farther inland.

The sea was near, and there were people living surprisingly close by, but Mai was in a place governed by the laws of another world.

The tide was at its fullest, she figured: it would begin to recede now. It didn't matter. Life and death were not at odds; they coexisted snugly right where she was.

Mai gave a wan laugh and looked around at the darkness the baby had left behind, and allowed herself to think about its future.

She hoped, of course, that morning would come soon, but she had a feeling that night would continue for quite some time yet. She wasn't sure if her consciousness could hold out until dawn.

Suddenly she had the feeling that the stars had come right down close to her. Or was it that her body had started to float? It didn't feel too bad.

Death was almost there.

# LEMON HEART

**1**

*November 1990*

.............................................................., and
his dream was set in a theater, one that seated about four
hundred people, the kind he was so used to, and had been
for so long. He wasn't in the audience seating or onstage,
but in a sound booth overlooking the stage from behind
the seats; evidently he was in charge of sound effects. In
front of him, illuminated by a work light, were the mixer
in its cabinet and a reel-to-reel tape deck. He was seated
on a chair, the index finger of his right hand on the tape
recorder's play button and his left hand on the mixer, ad-
justing sound levels; his gaze was fixed on the play onstage. He knew, all too well, that this was a dream. And
he knew, roughly, what was going to happen next, if he
didn't wake up first, which didn't look like it was going
to happen...and it was this self-awareness that he found
so mystifying. He couldn't figure out what to call this
neither/nor state he was in, as he crossed and recrossed
the border between sleep and wakefulness.

The sound booth was located next to the lighting
booth. It played an important role in supporting and in-
tensifying the drama unfolding onstage. His job was to

49

watch the progress of the play and provide music and sound effects at just the right moments, in response to signals from the stage director and in synch with the lighting man. This troupe was quite particular about how the music was handled. The actors' movements and lines were meant to match the rhythms of the songs he provided, so if his timing on the start button was off, it would ruin the whole play. They required constant concentration from their soundman: he wasn't able to relax, even for a moment, until the play was over.

Onstage, his favorite actress was performing, with great earnestness, the part she'd at long last landed. It was her debut—her career as an actress depended on each one of these precious moments, and she was savoring them.

He liked her personally, which only made him more determined to get the sound cues exactly right. His every thought was concentrated on the finger that would press play. He could feel sweat beading on his fingertip.

The music would play, and she'd sing a snippet of song: that was how the scene went. He'd push the play button, and from the speaker in front of the stage would come the sound, a snippet that he'd recorded and edited himself. That was what was supposed to happen.

He pressed play.

But what came from the speaker was no sound he'd ever heard before. Not only was it not music, it was too creepy even for one of their sound effects. Though he could hardly make it out, he thought it sounded like someone moaning—when the scene called for a cheerful little song. It was more than enough to destroy the play.

He watched the tape reel spin. It was his tape, the one he'd put together: no doubt about that. And he knew exactly what sounds were on it, and where. This keening wail was totally unforeseen.

*Who the hell put this on here?*

There was no time to think of a solution. Doubt assailed him from every side, and in his panic he allowed an effect scheduled for the next scene to play now. The ringing of a telephone echoed through the theater. The situation was beyond salvaging now.

The actress was young and inexperienced, and she couldn't improvise her way out of the situation. She simply stopped and looked up at the sound booth. With the house lights down and the booth's work light on, she'd be able to see him from the stage.

She looked up at him with a weapon-like clarity of gaze, and an accusatory gleam began to come into her eyes.

*How dare you ruin my debut like this!*

He gave up. He had no explanation for how those moans had gotten there. There was no way he was to blame—if anything, he was the victim. But he couldn't even voice his excuses: his body had stiffened, and he couldn't move. It felt like sleep paralysis.

Now all the actors onstage had stopped performing and were looking up at the sound booth. Audience members, too, following the actors' gazes, were beginning to turn around in their seats, half standing up to stare at him. His whole body felt the force of their recriminations.

*It's not my fault! It's not my fault!*

He didn't speak the words aloud, but somehow the microphone picked up the voice in his head and amplified it until it resounded throughout the theater.

"It's not my fault! It's not my fault!"

This attempt at self-vindication, more like a desperate cry, only poured oil on the flames. The crowd's reproach reached an even higher pitch, engulfing the hall.

But the sharpest gaze of all belonged to the young actress making her first appearance on a stage. The woman who had joined the troupe at the same time as him, with whom he'd done odd jobs together when they were interns, the woman with whom he'd exchanged encouraging words, the woman who had gradually become the object of his affections... He wanted to help her. He couldn't. Far from it: he was dragging her down. All he wanted, and he wanted it from the bottom of his heart, was for her to succeed as an actress, and now he was stealing that future from her, and all he could do was gnash his teeth... He could say he loved her all he wanted, but in reality it all came down to this.

Clutching at his chest, drowning in sweat, Toyama awoke from his dream.

For the first few minutes after waking up from the dream, he didn't know where he was. Then, as he got his breathing under control and looked around, Toyama began to grasp the situation. Mirrored ceiling, a circular bed that wasn't his, a woman in a towel sitting next to that oversized bed...

He tried to look up at her, and suddenly his chest hurt like it was being squeezed. He shivered; he could feel a cold sweat break out on his back. His chest and back had been giving him a lot of pain lately; this time, too, it made him uneasy. *Not again*, he thought; maybe he ought to see a doctor after all.

"You were having a nightmare."

She flashed him a playful smile, as if he'd shown her something really amusing.

Toyama groaned and lay there supine and motionless for a time. He was afraid that if he made the wrong move now he'd get dizzy and fall over. He waited for his breathing to relax.

At length he gingerly rolled over on the bed. He might be alright.

He quietly separated himself from the woman, weighing what he'd dreamed against what he knew to be real; he heaved a sigh. How many times had he dreamed terrifying things, knowing all the while that it was a dream? And each time, even knowing it for what it was, he cowered before the same dream, and then felt relief when he was able to confirm it wasn't real.

He looked at his watch and asked the woman, "Hey, how long have I been asleep?"

"Fifteen minutes, maybe? I saw you were asleep and

went to take a shower. When I got back, you were having a nightmare. You're being punished for all the bad stuff you do, don't you think?"

Toyama gave a bitter smile and buried his face in the pillow. He had more than an inkling of what she was talking about. Here he was, forty-seven, married, a father, and he was still fooling around. No doubt the woman assumed his wife must've found out and confronted him, and thus the cold sweat.

He wasn't drunk. It wasn't even night. It was two in the afternoon. Once they left the hotel they'd be under the clear blue skies of late November. He'd had a little lull at work, so he'd called up an old flame under the pretense of doing lunch; they'd gone to a hotel; sated from food and sex, and tired from accumulated fatigue, he'd suddenly been overcome by sleep; and in those few minutes, that fragmentary dream... It wasn't hard to assign it meaning. The same dream had tormented him over and over as a twenty-three-year-old college student. That was twenty-four years ago.

The dream came in lots of variations. Sometimes, he'd be sitting in the sound booth cuing the tape, which he'd mended with adhesive tape, and it would break, with an audible snap. Sometimes the tape would produce a strange noise unconnected with the scene onstage. What all the variants had in common was the fact that his actions produced some sound that ruined the performance of the woman he loved just as she was going to make her stage debut.

He'd had that nightmare twenty-four years ago. At the time he'd been manning the sound booth for Theater Group Soaring: it had been an all-too-plausible scenario then, and in fact something along those lines had actually happened to him.

But he hadn't had the dream for twenty-four years—why was it back now? He thought he knew the answer to that.

The guy's business card was still in his card-case. *Kenzo Yoshino, Daily News, Yokosuka Branch Office.*

It was a month now since this Yoshino guy had called him up out of the blue. A weekday afternoon. Toyama had just come back from lunch and sat down at his desk. He answered the phone himself. The caller, this Yoshino, had first confirmed Toyama's name and the fact that in 1965 he had been a member of Theater Group Soaring, and then he'd taken a deep breath and said, *I'd like to ask you a few questions about Sadako Yamamura, if I may.*

Toyama remembered Yoshino's voice distinctly: it was that of a man struggling against panic, grasping at straw. And it was no wonder the man's voice had left such an impression, considering what he'd said. Toyama had never met the man, but he was talking about Sadako Yamamura, a woman whose name Toyama hadn't heard anyone utter for twenty-four years, as often as he might recall it in secret to himself. Every time he thought of her face his chest tightened and his pulse quickened. Obviously, he wasn't over her yet, even all these years later.

Yoshino said he wanted to get together and talk with him about Sadako. Toyama agreed to meet him once. He couldn't pass up the chance, considering how much the subject interested him, too. He arranged to meet Yoshino in a coffee shop in Akasaka, near his office.

Yoshino looked every inch the old-time reporter as, stroking his beard, he tried to coax forth Toyama's distant memories. He concentrated on the time immediately surrounding Sadako's disappearance.

*Sadako Yamamura went missing in 1966, right after a Soaring performance, correct?*

Yoshino was very persistent about wanting to know her movements after leaving the troupe. He didn't rush, and he paused between each question, but his vocal and facial expressions betrayed the depth of his interest in Sadako.

*What happened to Sadako twenty-four years ago?* How was Toyama to know? He'd searched for her himself, desperately. If ever he'd found out where Sadako had disappeared to, his life now would be very different.

And so he knew exactly why the nightmare was back. It was all due to Yoshino, his mention of Sadako's name. It was the only thing that could have brought back those dreams, and all the suffering they had caused him.

# 2

They emerged from the hotel into glaring sunlight. The harsh light bothered him—or was it his conscience, after what he'd done in that room? Quite a contrast to the mild signs of late autumn all around them.

They walked quickly up the sidewalk to a place where the crowd thinned out. Toyama clasped the woman's hand and muttered, "Well, gotta go."

"Back to the office?" she replied, with an untroubled smile. She took one hand from her hip and waved. Goodbye.

"I've got a ton of work to catch up on."

"But in spite of that, you just couldn't control this," she said, gesturing as if to grab his crotch. "You never could."

It suddenly occurred to Toyama that it might be time to quit this. He wasn't young anymore, and there was no telling when one of his attacks might turn life-threatening.

"I'll give you a call," he said, blowing her a little kiss and turning away. After walking a bit, he turned to look back: she was still watching him. He waved, then hurried through the Nogizaka neighborhood toward Hitotsugi Street. When he'd said he had a ton of work to catch up on, it was no lie.

In his junior year of college he'd suddenly taken it into his head to become a playwright. That was how he'd come to join Theater Group Soaring's production department. So far so good, but it turned out that there were so many good writers and directors in the group who were senior to him that he knew he'd never get a chance to show what he was capable of. Placed in charge of music, he learned the job and then went back to school, graduating a year late. He lucked into a job at a record company, where he became a project director; he'd been doing it for twenty-three years now. The job was just something that had allowed him to utilize his experience with theater sound, but once he'd gotten into it he found it a fascinating line of work—he came to look at it as a calling.

It was a fun job, as long as he was in the studio involved with recording. He'd never once found that part of the job unpleasant. Sometimes he hated attending planning meetings with executives, but dealing with musicians gave him virtually no stress at all. All in all he felt it was a job worth doing, and he was glad he'd found it. Not only that, but the industry as a whole was healthy, and things looked like they were only going to get better. Things were bullish in every respect, his salary was all he could wish for, and he never lacked for female company. Toyama had no complaints about the situation he found himself in. Even the work that now awaited him back at the office was fundamentally something he enjoyed. He had no worries, other than, lately, some physical problems.

But he had to admit that hearing Yoshino mention Sadako Yamamura, and now dreaming about her again, unsettled him in ways he couldn't quite pin down. Sadako, it was fair to say, was the only woman in the world for him. He'd botched his first marriage. The second one was more stable, and they had kids. Surrounded by children and a wife too young for him, he had a satisfying life now—but he often wondered "what if."

*What would have happened if Sadako and I had gotten married?*

That wasn't the only "if" that occurred to him.

*If the end of the world came, who would I want to be with?*

*If I could do it all over, who would I spend my life with?*

*If I could only make love to a woman once in my life, who would it be?*

The answer to all these questions, for Toyama, was Sadako. If she appeared before him this very instant and offered to accept him, he'd be prepared to give up anything and everything. He even thought he'd be willing to die, if he could only touch her skin once more.

*I've got to call.*

If he could catch up on his work today, he'd have quite a bit of free time tomorrow, November 27th. It wouldn't be too much trouble to go down to Yokosuka if he was asked to.

He decided it would be better to call from a pay phone than from the office, so he walked to the edge of the sidewalk and took out a telephone card and the

59

man's business card. He punched the number for the Yokosuka Branch Office of the *Daily News*. Kenzo Yoshino himself answered.

Their last conversation had been pretty one-sided, with Yoshino asking all the questions. He'd seemed to be in a hurry, and had given only the most rudimentary replies to Toyama's inquiries. As soon as he'd learned what he wanted to know, or realized that he could get no further information from Toyama, Yoshino had cut their meeting short, getting up and walking out. It had left Toyama with a myriad of questions, and the feeling that Yoshino's behavior had been inconsiderate, to say the least.

*Why was a reporter sniffing around after Sadako anyway?*

That was the most obvious question, and now it was whirling around in his head. Toyama briefly explained to Yoshino what he wanted to know and asked, politely, if they could get together and talk.

He added that if he needed to he'd be willing to go down to Yokosuka, but Yoshino said that wouldn't be necessary, and he explained his schedule for tomorrow. A colleague from the *Daily News* had died the day before in a Shinagawa hospital, and Yoshino was planning to go up to Shinagawa for the funeral. He said he could meet him for an hour or so after the funeral.

*Let's meet at four o'clock at Shinbaba Station on the Keihin Express line, at the ticket gate.*

Toyama repeated the time and place, wrote them in his schedule book, and hung up.

# 3

The sun was quick in setting today. Toward late afternoon the sky darkened as if shrouded in mist and the sun sank with violent rapidity. The air grew markedly chill, and it felt like winter as he stood by the ticket gate, which opened into a shopping street.

Toyama and Yoshino were both there five minutes early.

Yoshino looked more careworn and forlorn than he had a month before. Of course, he'd just come from a junior colleague's funeral—that probably had something to do with it. When someone younger dies, it's always depressing.

Toyama had never gotten out at this station before. He knew that if he walked east he'd eventually run into a canal, and before that he'd hit the Shore Road, running north and south. On the water side of that was a quiet warehouse district, where overhead one could hear the horns of shipping in Tokyo Bay.

Toyama and Yoshino walked together to a coffee shop just this side of the Shore Road. They went inside and ordered coffee, but before they'd had time to exchange more than a few words, Yoshino's pager went off. He left the table and went to the pink pay phone in the back of the shop. Toyama watched him from behind. Yoshino looked every inch the reporter as he cradled the receiver on his shoulder and dialed.

Toyama had no difficulty overhearing Yoshino's end of the conversation.

"What? Mai Takano's been found dead?"

*Mai Takano...* Of course Toyama had never heard the name before. All he was interested in was what happened to Sadako. He couldn't muster any interest in this woman whose name he didn't recognize. He tried to ignore the rest of the conversation.

Yoshino made no effort to muffle his voice as he bent over the receiver and barked out questions. The somewhat sad expression of a moment before was gone now, and Yoshino was once again the reporter sniffing out a story. He looked reenergized.

"Three days ago... Where? ...East Shinagawa—wait a minute, that's not far from where I am now. I could swing by if I have time... Which was it? You know, was it a forensic autopsy or an administrative one? I see... Hmm, ninety hours after time of death.... Huh? Signs that she gave birth just prior to death? ...the umbilical cord? Are you kidding me? And what about the baby? ...Gone? You mean...hide nor hair?"

It was enough for Toyama to piece together the situation. Three days ago a woman named Mai Takano had been found dead in this vicinity. An autopsy had been performed, revealing that she'd given birth immediately before her death. And the child was now missing.

A shocking incident, to be sure. But after all, it had nothing to do with him. It didn't matter to him who had died and how, or what she'd given birth to—or even if that newborn baby had, totally under its own power (strange though that would be), disappeared...

Toyama thought—was determined to think—that the incident had no connection with him, and yet his nerves were tingling.

*Mai Takano.*

He'd never heard the name before. So why did he now feel like it was engraved somewhere deep in his heart?

He found himself imagining her body, already entering rigor mortis, with something squirming beside it. Imagining an infant climbing over its mother's corpse and walking away.

A chill came over him. He had a powerful intuition regarding what Mai Takano had given birth to, and it wouldn't let him tell himself anymore that he wasn't interested. As he watched Yoshino hunched over the phone and listened to the unguarded fragments of his conversation, the facts, or pieces of them, began to form definite images in his brain and play themselves out. It was like when he took segments of music and edited them together into a single, smoothly flowing track.

Toyama closed his eyes and turned his face to the ceiling. The voice at the phone stopped and there was a moment of silence. When he opened his eyes again, Yoshino was seated opposite him—when had he returned? The last few minutes, the duration of the phone call, felt distorted to Toyama—forcefully so, like he'd been twisted up and tossed abruptly into another dimension.

"Is there something wrong?" Yoshino sounded concerned by the look of enervated astonishment on Toyama's face.

Toyama straightened up in his seat—he'd sunk into a slouch—and took a deep breath before saying, "No... But it sounds like you've got quite a sensational incident on your hands."

"I don't know about that yet. A young female was found dead on a rooftop, is all."

"Nearby?"

"Yeah, East Shinagawa. An office building. She was found in the exhaust shaft on the roof—a hole, basically. Odd, right?"

"Was it murder?"

"It doesn't sound like it. Probably an accident."

"I didn't mean to eavesdrop, but, um, I heard you say that there were signs she'd given birth just before dying."

Yoshino gave Toyama an indecipherable grin and a questioning glance. *Why are you so interested in this?*

"Well, I don't know anything yet—I just heard the report. A pity it had to happen to someone so young, though. She was a smart girl. Pretty, too."

Yoshino looked away and stroked his beard. There seemed to be something more bothering him. Toyama had a hunch.

"This Mai Takano—she didn't happen to be an acquaintance of yours?"

Yoshino immediately shook his head. "No, I didn't know her personally. But a colleague of mine did, Asakawa. It was his funeral I was at: we were pretty close. He knew her."

A look of anxiety crossed Yoshino's face, and Toyama observed it. Anxiety—but more than that, dread.

"Their deaths—were they just a coincidence?"

At the question, Yoshino's dread deepened, and Toyama saw that too.

First his friend Asakawa dies, and now a girl Asakawa knew. Neither death in itself terribly suspicious, but precisely because there was so little information, it was natural for an outsider to want to connect them.

Yoshino's eyes began darting around the room, as if he were desperately coming up with ideas and rejecting them.

"Yeah, right... Now, about Sadako Yamamura."

Yoshino changed the subject, but the way he said it made it seem almost as if Sadako had something to do with Asakawa's and Mai's deaths.

The last time Toyama and Yoshino had met, Toyama had simply answered the questions put to him. That had been his role, and he'd played it to the hilt, but he had no intention of reprising it. This time he was determined to take the initiative and find out why a reporter was so interested in ascertaining what had happened to Sadako.

So he came right out and said it. "Don't you think it's about time you told me why you want to know what she was doing twenty-four years ago?"

Yoshino hung his head and looked beaten—it was the same look he'd had the last time they'd met.

"See, the thing is...I don't really know myself."

That was what he'd said last time, too. Toyama couldn't accept it. A reporter for a major news organization follows a woman's quarter-century-old trail through the nooks and crannies of the city, and he doesn't even know why?

"Don't give me that." Toyama's expression began to change.

Yoshino raised his hands and said, "Okay. I'll be honest with you. Kazuyuki Asakawa, a reporter in the main office, was investigating something, and Sadako Yamamura's name came up. He needed information. But he was tied up elsewhere at the time, so he asked me to help him out. He told me to find out whatever I could about what Sadako Yamamura was doing twenty-four years ago."

Toyama leaned forward. "What was he investigating?"

"That's the thing. He never told me. And then he got in a traffic accident and went into a coma. He died without ever regaining consciousness. I don't know why he was so insistent about finding out about her. I guess the truth is lost in a grove—like in that movie, you know?"

Toyama peered deep into Yoshino's eyes, trying to tell if he was lying. He didn't seem to be, at least about the big stuff. But he might be lying about the details.

Toyama deduced how Yoshino had been led to him. First he would have gone to Theater Group Soaring's rehearsal space, where he would have found out who else had joined the troupe as an intern in February of 1965. The resumes they'd all submitted together with their entrance exams were still stored in the troupe's offices. As far as Toyama could recall, there had been eight of them that year. No doubt Yoshino had thought he could trace Sadako's steps by speaking to all of them.

"Did you talk to the others?"

Toyama could only remember the names of two or three others, besides Sadako. He had no contact with any of them now—no idea where they were or what they were doing.

"Of the people who joined Soaring in 1965, I was able to track down four, including yourself."

"So you were able to contact the other three as well?"

Yoshino nodded. "I talked to them on the phone."

"Who?"

"Iino, Kitajima, and Kato."

As Yoshino said the names, Toyama was able to recall the faces. They'd been slumbering in the recesses of his memory; now he could feel them coming back to him, more clearly by the moment. Of course, in his mind, everyone still looked twenty.

Iino: he'd completely forgotten about Iino. Didn't speak much; a skilled mime. The older girls had liked him: they'd kind of adopted him.

Kitajima: small, not much stage presence, but he was good with his lines. He'd been used as a narrator, impressive for an intern. Toyama thought he'd had a slight crush on Sadako, too.

Kato: her first name was Keiko, he remembered now. Her name had been so ordinary that Shigemori, their director and head of the troupe, had given her a flashy stage name. "Yurako Tatsunomiya." She was quite beautiful, and she certainly wasn't aiming for comic roles, which was what such an overwrought name might have steered her toward. Still, the name was a direct gift from the troupe's founder-director, and she couldn't very well turn it down. Toyama remembered how hard a time she'd had hiding her mixed feelings. They'd all be out drinking, and people would start mocking the name, which would leave her near tears as she tried to defend it.

In fact, it was Sadako who probably wanted a stage name most. Her real name was too old-fashioned for a modern beauty like hers. She should have received a stage name when she first went on stage, last-minute though it was. But Shigemori had sent her on under her real name.

All these things about people Toyama thought he'd forgotten came vividly back as Yoshino said their names. He began to wax nostalgic. But just as he was on the point of losing himself in the feelings of his youth, he dug in his heels. He had another question to ask.

"So you only talked to Iino, Kitajima, and Kato on the phone?" *Why was I the only one you met face-to-face?*

"I called you first, too, you know."

"I know that. What I mean is, you let it go at a phone call for the other three, but you wanted to meet me in person. Why?"

Yoshino studied Toyama with a surprised look. His expression said, *Do you even have to ask?*

"I thought you knew. The other three all said the same thing, that you and Sadako had a special relationship back then."

*A special relationship.*

He felt his strength leave him, and he sank down into his seat again. From this position he could see stains on the ceiling.

"Is that it..."

It made sense now. No wonder Yoshino had wanted to meet him in person, instead of just talking on the phone like with the other three.

He'd always meant to hide his closeness to Sadako from the other interns, not to mention the troupe as a whole. But it now seemed that his fellow interns had seen right through him. So much so that they still remembered it twenty-four years later. He and Sadako must have made quite an impression. But Toyama couldn't believe there was anything all that memorable about himself, which meant it must have been Sadako's striking character that they remembered. Unless they'd really all been that intrigued by their relationship.

"Would you be willing to tell me what happened?"

Toyama lowered his gaze to find Yoshino staring at him with eyes brimming with curiosity.

"What do you mean?"

"Sadako Yamamura disappeared all of a sudden after the spring production in 1966 finished its run. I think you know why."

Toyama realized what Yoshino was thinking: if anybody would know why Sadako had left, he would, even if he didn't know where she'd gone. Yoshino had a hungry-wolf glint in his eyes.

"You've got to be kidding."

Toyama had nothing to give this predator. If he'd known why she left him, without telling him where she was going, his life since age twenty-three wouldn't have been so dark and cheerless.

"Oh, right. Shall I show you something?"

Yoshino rummaged in his briefcase and came up with a script. The battered cover read:

THEATER GROUP SOARING
ELEVENTH PRODUCTION
*GIRL IN BLACK*
(TWO ACTS, FOUR SCENES)
WRITTEN AND DIRECTED BY
YUSAKU SHIGEMORI

It was a copy of the bound galley of the script.

Toyama reached for it in spite of himself. He opened it. It smelled like twenty-four years ago.

"Where did you get this?" He asked without thinking.

"I borrowed it from the troupe's office, after swearing I'd return it. In March of 1966, Sadako Yamamura snagged a part as an understudy in this. Her disappearance was more or less simultaneous with the end of the run. What happened? It has to have had something to do with the play..."

"Have you read it?"

"Of course I have. But it's just the script: it doesn't tell me much."

Toyama began flipping through the pages. Twenty-four years ago he'd owned a copy of this. It was probably in one of his bookshelves now, but then again he'd no doubt lost it in one of the many moves that had accompanied his first marriage and divorce. No. No matter how he searched, this was something he'd never find at home.

The staff's names were written on the first page.

*Sound: Hiroshi Toyama.*

Finding his own name there gave him a weird, ticklish sort of feeling, as if he'd come face to face with his twenty-three-year-old self.

Next came the names of the cast.

*The Girl in Black: Aiko Hazuki.*

But Aiko Hazuki's name had been crossed out, and next to it somebody had written in ballpoint pen the name "Sadako Yamamura."

The girl who held the key to the story hadn't been given a name. Despite her importance, she didn't appear on stage all that much, although her few appearances had been designed for maximum impact. The part had originally belonged to Aiko Hazuki, one of the troupe's mid-ranked actresses. However, mere days before the first performance, Hazuki had collapsed, ill; Sadako, who had been attending every rehearsal as Hazuki's prompter, was asked to step in for her. It was to be her stage debut.

Thinking about it now, it seemed almost as if Shigemori had written the script especially for Sadako, as if under her inducement, even though she was nothing but an intern. At the time, of course, such a thought would never have crossed Toyama's mind. But when he considered her character and her image, unfaded in his mind after all these years, it almost seemed more plausible to think that Shigemori had written the part intending to cast her in it. The Girl in Black was that perfect for Sadako.

He turned the page. This seemed to be Shigemori's own copy of the script: the spaces between the lines of dialogue and stage directions were crammed with performance notes and critiques of the actors' performances, all in cramped handwriting. There were even details regarding the timing of the sound effects.

*M1—Theme song.*

The curtain rises. A living room set occupies stage center. The lights come up gradually, and the set begins to brighten.

.........

.........

*M5—Distant church bells. Mixed in, the sound of many footsteps, the noise of a crowd.*

This was the Girl in Black's first scene. Following a sound effect cue, she was to appear onstage for just an instant.

Unconsciously, Toyama was tapping the tabletop with his right index finger.

*Play button—on.*

The tape spun, the sound effect began. The Girl in Black was supposed to step onto the stage in synch with the sound.

The Girl in Black: an ill omen. She wasn't to be visible from every seat in the house: from some points you wouldn't be able to see her because of where she was standing. She'd be onstage, but only some people would know it. But that was okay: it was part of the effect of the play.

Toyama could see her again vividly. She was eighteen. The only woman he'd ever loved, the woman he couldn't forget even now...

Without meaning to, Toyama spoke her name.

# 4

*March 1966*

It was full-dress rehearsal day for Theater Group Soaring's eleventh production. Toyama had shut himself up in the sound booth to make his final adjustments. Tomorrow was opening day, and he was checking his tapes and equalizers to make sure everything was as it should be; even now, all alone in front of the control board, he was enjoying his job. He caught himself whistling. After two months of rehearsals, they'd been able to formally move into the theater—excitement was winning out even over the nervousness of opening. All throughout rehearsals he'd had Shigemori sitting next to him giving him detailed orders concerning the sound, and when he failed to follow instructions absolutely to the letter, Shigemori had bawled him out mercilessly. The director couldn't tolerate a second's delay in a sound effect or a slight discrepancy in volume. Day after day of pressure had begun to take a toll on his stomach... But now the sound booth was his castle, his independent kingdom. The director rarely looked in, and as long as Toyama got the timing right with the tapes, he got no complaints. Once a play got underway the director's attention was always riveted to the stage—he paid so little attention to the sound that Toyama would actually begin to wonder what all the fuss had been about. Knowing this idiosyncrasy of Shigemori's, Toyama had eagerly anticipated his move into the theater's sound booth.

It wasn't as if he were utterly free from anxiety—he had nightmares about an unplanned sound getting through—but he knew that couldn't happen, so as a worry it was nothing compared to the pressure the director's presence had brought to bear on him. It was only a dream...kind of amusing, really.

Toyama's sound booth was at the top of a spiral staircase leading up from the lobby, right next to the lighting booth. There was no way to get directly to it from the stage area, so anyone coming from the green room or backstage had to first go out to the lobby and then up the stairs. There was an intercom connection with the backstage area, so communication was easy enough, but once the doors had been opened actually going back and forth became quite troublesome. Maybe that was why Shigemori seemed to lose interest in the sound once the play started. In their rehearsal space, the director's chair was right next to the soundman's—an unfortunate circumstance that forced Toyama to bear a burden he otherwise would have been spared.

They finished unloading in the morning, spent the afternoon getting everything into place, and in the evening they were scheduled to have their final full-dress rehearsal. This, too, was easy on the soundman. All he had to carry in was his tape reels; he was spared the heavy labor of lugging in the props.

Once in a while Toyama would raise his head and look down at the busily transforming stage. On the other side of the soundproof glass, the set was almost complete. From this vantage he could see everybody working together to create a single finished product. It was something he enjoyed watching: it felt like a reward for the long, difficult rehearsals. He fancied that at that very moment the actors, with no particular job to do, were in the green room savoring the exact same feeling.

Toyama ate his dinner—they'd had it brought in—and then he set up his music reel and his sound effects reel and checked the sequence of cues. No problems at all. All that was left now was to wait for the dress rehearsal to begin. After it was finished, they'd get together for a final round of feedback, and then break for the night. The theater had a strict closing time, so there would be no midnight rehearsals tonight. For him, moving into the theater also meant freedom from having to stick around for late rehearsals, worrying about missing his last train home.

Suddenly Toyama sensed a presence behind him. He turned around.

The door was ajar, and a woman was standing just outside it. In the dim light of the booth he couldn't make out her face. Toyama got up and opened the door wider.

"Oh, Sada. It's you."

Sadako Yamamura stood in the doorway blankly. Toyama took her hand and brought her into the booth, shutting the door again behind her. The door was heavy, soundproof.

He waited for her to say something, but she just stared past him, tight-lipped, at the almost-complete stage below. The living room set was being assembled, and the director was giving detailed instructions regarding the placement of its various components.

"I'm afraid."

The words resonated with all the naïve simplicity of an aspiring actress facing her first appearance onstage. Sadako had graduated from high school on the island of Izu Oshima and immediately come up to Tokyo; she'd made a remarkably rapid transition from intern to actress. She had every right to be nervous and uneasy. Needless to say, out of the eight interns, she was the only one going onstage tonight.

Toyama tried to encourage her. "Don't worry. I'll be cheering for you up here."

Sadako shook her head. "That's not what I mean."

Her gaze was hollow as she shifted it from the stage to the spinning tape reel. It was blank—he'd just checked it, but he'd neglected to push *stop*, so on it spun.

Toyama stopped it and rewound it.

"Everybody's scared when they debut," he said over the sound of the tape rewinding. But Sadako's reply was strangely off, like an out-of-focus picture.

"Hey, is there a woman's voice on that tape?"

Toyama laughed. As far as he could recall, he'd never recorded a solo human voice: playing something like that while an actor was delivering his lines would kill the performance. Under normal circumstances they'd never overlay dialogue with dialogue like that.

"What kind of question is that, out of the blue?"

"It's something Okubo said a few minutes ago, you know, when you were checking your sound levels. He made a funny face, like he was afraid of something. He said there was a woman's voice on the tape. Not only that, he said he'd heard it before. So I..."

Okubo was another one of the interns, multitalented but short, and so sensitive about it that it had given him a complex of sorts. He was another one who had a crush on Sadako.

"I know what you're talking about. That's crowd noise. You know, what we play in the background during your scene."

They'd taken the crowd noise for that scene from a movie. The voices were just supposed to be submerged in the background; no one voice was supposed to be heard above the others. But it might be possible for someone to have the auditory illusion that he or she was hearing one of them in particular, in an aural close-up, as it were.

"No, that's not it." Her denial was forceful enough to bother Toyama.

"Well, then, do you know what scene it was?"

If he could figure out where it was on the tape, he

could check it now on the headphones. If there was a strange woman's voice on there, he had to deal with it now, or it would be trouble later.

But the chances of that were next to nil. He couldn't count the number of times he'd listened to the tape during rehearsals. Not to mention the repeated scrutiny he'd given it on his headphones when he'd edited it together. There was no way a stray sound could have gotten on there at this point.

"Okubo's been saying strange things. You know that little Shinto altar backstage?"

"Most playhouses have 'em."

Toyama was beginning to guess what Okubo must have been telling Sadako. Just as theaters all had Shinto altars, they all had scary stories whispered about them. Handling the set pieces and props allowed for lots of accidents and injuries, and wherever actors gathered there were bound to be vortices of ill feeling—as a result there probably wasn't a theater around without one or two spook tales. Okubo had probably been scaring Sadako with some nonsense like that. In which case, her insistence on there being a woman's voice on the tape was probably groundless.

"No, there's another one."

"Another what?"

"Altar."

Toyama had seen the altar himself any number of times, set into the concrete wall stage left, at the back. But that was the only one he knew of.

"Where?"

Still standing in front of the door, Sadako raised her left hand and pointed. The spot she indicated was behind the table. Toyama couldn't see it from where he was. But all of a sudden a chill ran down his spine. This room was his castle: he liked to think he knew what was where. There couldn't be an altar here.

He started to get up.

She giggled. "Startled?"

"Don't scare me like that!" He sat back down. The chair felt cold somehow.

"Come on, it's over here." Sadako took Toyama's hand and pulled him out of his chair, seating herself in front of a cabinet built into the wall. A pair of doors were set into the wall about ten centimeters from the floor; they opened outward. Sadako looked from Toyama to the doors, as if suggesting he open them.

A storage space. He hadn't expected one. The doors were about fifty centimeters square. There were no handles, so they blended in with the rest of the wall, and he hadn't noticed them.

He placed a finger in the center of the doors, pressed, and released. The doors opened without a sound. He'd expected to find old tape reels and cords piled randomly inside, but what he found was something rather different. Two metal shelves, on the upper of which sat two rows of tapes in carefully labeled boxes. No doubt leftovers from previous productions. The bottom shelf contained a little wooden box that looked, just as Sadako had said, like an altar.

All he'd done was open those two little doors, but the atmosphere in the sound booth was utterly changed. A foreign space had suddenly opened up right next to the table he was so accustomed to working at. He wasn't sure whether there was actually a smell or not, but Toyama at least had the illusion that his nose detected the scent of rotting meat.

Toyama sat down next to Sadako, in front of the altar, hugging his knees. There was an offering in front of the altar, right in front of his nose now. It was a desiccated and wrinkled thing no bigger than the tip of his little finger, and at first he thought it was a shriveled piece of burdock.

Without a hint of hesitation, Sadako picked up the piece of whatever-it-was and placed it in Toyama's hand, as if giving him a piece of candy.

Toyama allowed himself to be led along. He accepted the offering on the palm of his hand and studied it.

He only realized what it was when Sadako brought her nose close to his palm and sniffed it. Suddenly a thought wedged its way into his brain. Not just a thought—a woman's voice, whispering.

*The baby's coming.*

In a flash, Toyama understood.

*It's an umbilical cord. A baby's umbilical cord.*

There was no mistaking it now: it was indeed an umbilical cord, severed long ago.

The instant he realized it, Toyama jumped back from the altar, flinging the thing in his hand at Sadako. She caught it and said, calmly, as if to herself, "Looks like Okubo was right."

Toyama slowly brought his breathing under control, trying not to appear too foolish in front of a younger woman. Feigning calm, he asked, "What do you mean?"

"About the woman's voice on the tape. He said he'd heard it before, moaning, like she was in pain. He said if he had to describe it, he'd say it sounded like she was suffering the pains of childbirth. That's what he said. And it looks like that woman had her baby."

Toyama didn't know how to respond to this. What Okubo had said was strange enough, but the way Sadako just coolly accepted it was way beyond eerie.

Just then the director's voice came over the intercom.

"Everybody, we're about to start dress rehearsal. Cast, staff, to your places, please."

The order was salvation to Toyama: he normally didn't look forward to hearing Shigemori's voice, but now it sounded like a god's. It had power enough to drag him immediately back to reality, certainly.

Sadako had to report to her position onstage. She couldn't stay here talking nonsense.

"Hey, you're on. Break a leg," he managed to say, though his throat was dry and his voice scratchy. He placed a hand on her back and urged her toward the stage. Sadako squirmed as if reluctant and made a show of refusing to budge.

But then she said, "Okay, well, later, then."

There was something thrillingly suggestive about the way she said it, and the way she looked when she said it. Toyama thought he could see her maturing as an actress right before his eyes. Five years younger than him, in Toyama's eyes she was the very incarnation of cute. Instead of the sensuality of a grown woman, she still had the innocence of a girl: that was what attracted him, what he was madly in love with. But now she seemed so sensuous...

Toyama forgot himself as he watched Sadako descend the spiral staircase.

Since the dress rehearsal would proceed exactly like a real performance, he'd be playing the tapes from start to finish. If there was a foreign noise on there, this would be a good chance to locate it.

Toyama put on his headphones and tried to concentrate on his cues. But he was distracted by the proximity of the cabinet with the altar in it. The director hadn't yet given the sign to start. The house was dark; the sound booth was illuminated only by the work light on the table.

He stole a glance sideways. The cabinet doors were half open. Evidently he hadn't shut them tightly enough.

*The voice of a woman in childbirth? Of all the stupid things.*

Without taking off his headphones, Toyama moved over and pushed the cabinet door with his foot. He did it with his foot in order to show that he wasn't scared.

He heard a distinct click as the doors shut. But at that very moment, in his headphones, he heard a faint voice. It was weak, a baby's voice. He couldn't tell if it was crying or laughing...or maybe it had just been born...

Toyama stared at the tape. It wasn't moving.

The director gave the sign, and the curtain rose. He was supposed to provide the opening theme now, but his trembling hand slipped on the play button more than once, and he was late with it. He'd get a chewing-out later, not that he cared about that now.

*Play button, on.*

The baby's voice was gone, drowned out by the bouncy opening theme.

As Toyama sat there bathed in cold sweat, trying to figure out where the sound had come from, his nostrils detected a mild scent that reminded him of lemons.

## 5

The first act ended, and everybody was given a twenty-minute break except the actors the director wanted to scold. Toyama was afraid he'd be taken to task for being late with the opening theme, but no mention was made of it, and he was able to leave the sound booth for a time.

He descended to the lobby. Passing the concession kiosk he jogged down the hallway toward the actors' green room. He didn't have long. He wasn't sure there was enough time to grab Okubo and find out what he wanted to...

He burst into the big space used as a green room. When he saw that Okubo wasn't there he turned to a senior member of the troupe who was practicing lines in front of a mirror and said, "Sorry to disturb you, but do you know where I can find Okubo?"

The actor paused and stuck out his chin. "He's Arima's prompter, so I imagine he's with him, stage right."

"Thank you."

But in fact he nearly ran into Okubo as he went to leave the room. Okubo leaned over and jumped aside with exaggerated movements. "A thousand pardons," he said, putting on airs, speaking as if performing the role of an English gentleman. Okubo was like this: his every movement, his every pose, his every word was theatrical. He and Toyama were the same age, and so they ended up spending a lot of time together, and they got along fairly well. But sometimes Okubo's flair for the dramatic got on Toyama's nerves.

With a joyless smile, Toyama grabbed Okubo's sleeve and pulled him aside. "I need to talk to you."

"This is sudden. What about?" But Okubo's grin betrayed his lack of surprise.

"Why don't you have a seat?"

They grabbed chairs from in front of the mirror and sat down.

Okubo looked even smaller when sitting down. He kept his back and neck straight—his posture was perfect. In fact, Toyama never saw him slouch, or even really relax. No doubt this was a method of making up for his lack of height. Okubo took pride in the fact that before joining Soaring he'd belonged to a troupe with a considerably more celebrated heritage. Just being accepted there was a considerable feat, and he'd done it—but no more. Unable to make his way in that troupe, he'd bailed out and joined Soaring, which represented coming down a notch. Okubo had persuaded himself that it was only because of his height.

In short, Toyama knew full well that Okubo's comically exaggerated way of talking and moving came from a combination of pride and insecurity.

He only had twenty minutes, though: he decided to come right out with it.

"What nonsense have you been filling Sadako's head with?"

"Are you trying to ruin my reputation? I don't recall talking nonsense to anyone," came Okubo's composed, good-natured reply.

"Listen, I'm not accusing you of anything, but something's got me worried."

"What, pray tell?"

"Hey, sound effects and music are my job. I've got a right to be concerned. I want you to be honest with me: was what you told Sadako the truth? Did you really hear a woman's voice on the tape? A woman in the throes of labor?"

Okubo clapped his hands and laughed. "'A woman in the throes of labor'? Where did you come up with that? What I said was, it sounded like the act that results in labor pains—a woman's moans when, you know... That's what I meant, at least. I don't know what Sada thought I was talking about."

"So you were joking?"

"I was not joking," said Okubo, laughing again. He was so caught up in his own performance that it was hard to get a straight answer from him. What was he so keyed up about anyway?

"Stop fooling around, will you? I heard something."

"What?"

"A baby crying."

Okubo took a deep breath and then leaned forward, a look of concern on his face. "Where?"

"In the sound booth, over my headphones."

Okubo leaned back again. "Whoa." He looked taken aback.

"See, it connects. If you heard a woman struggling to deliver a child, see, it's too much of a coincidence." As he said this, Toyama was remembering the umbilical cord that had been placed as an offering in front of that altar.

"Why, that's a bolt from the blue! A horse of a different color!" said Okubo, in his best vaudevillian voice.

"Knock it off already. Can you just tell me what it was you told Sadako?"

"Sada's the one great hope for us interns. Between her beauty and the attention the director pays her, she's got a great future as an actress. But after all, it's her first performance—to a bystander like me, she looks incredibly nervous. I feel sorry for her. It was an act of fellowship, if you will. I thought I'd tell her a scary story or two, just to, you know, loosen her up a bit."

Annoyed, Toyama pressed the point. "So you didn't really hear a woman's voice on the tape?"

"*Au contraire!*" Okubo shook his head and pursed his lips.

"One more thing. How did you know there was an altar in the sound booth?"

"An altar? In the sound booth?" Okubo pulled a long face and clapped his hands as one does when worshipping at a shrine. He closed his eyes, bowed his head, and began mumbling as if reciting a sutra.

Toyama was finding Okubo even more grating than usual today. He sighed and continued. "Yes, an altar. A little one, about this big," he said, tracing its size in the air.

"I have never set foot inside yon sound booth."

"So you heard about it from someone else?"

"Well, I pray to the altar at stage left every day," Okubo replied, clapping his hands again.

"Okay, okay. So, you didn't tell Sadako about the altar."

"Not only didn't I tell her about it, I had no idea it was there myself."

*So how did Sadako know it was there?* She had claimed Okubo told her, but Okubo was saying he didn't know about it. S—one of them was lying? Okubo, at least, sounded like he was telling the truth.

Toyama pondered for a while.

*When Okubo said there was a woman's voice on the sound effects tape, he was just trying to frighten Sadako. Well, that's the kind of scary story you hear in any playhouse—nothing to get seriously angry about. Okubo told Sadako that he'd heard a woman moaning in pleasure—a woman engaged in sex. But for some reason she told me that it was the sound of a woman suffering in childbirth. Was it just a misunderstanding? But what about the umbilical cord? It fits too well.*

Toyama thought of what he'd heard in the headphones, that faint cry of an infant—he couldn't get it out of his head. He had to get back to the booth in time for the second act, but he was reluctant to go. He didn't want to be alone in there. He'd rather be here, under bright lights in the big room.

His gaze was hollow as he asked, "By the way, where's Sadako now?"

Suddenly Okubo was all informality. "Whaddya mean? Weren't you paying attention to the play? The Great Director kept her behind to give her direction. She's probably still onstage now, being put through the wringer."

Toyama had already forgotten. At the end of the first act he'd watched from the sound booth window as the director had instructed a few actors to line up on stage for feedback. He'd noticed Sadako among them. That's where she'd be now, listening to Shigemori tell her what was wrong with her performance and how she could have done it better.

From where he stood, it looked to Toyama like Shigemori paid Sadako an abnormal amount of atten-tion. He'd been shocked sometimes during rehearsals to see the way Shigemori looked at her—on the verge of tears, with an expression made up of equal parts love and hatred and a gaze so intense that no one acquainted with Shigemori would have believed it. Shigemori held ab-solute power within the troupe, so if he had his eye on someone it was a foregone conclusion that he'd be mak-ing physical advances. And of course that was something

Toyama, given his love for Sadako, would do anything to avert.

Just then Shigemori's voice came over the intercom.

"The second act will be starting soon. Places, everyone."

Toyama started to run, knowing how much distance separated the big room from his sound booth. So when Okubo spoke, it was to his back.

"Hey, Toyama, don't leave the intercom on in the sound booth anymore. We can hear everything you say in here."

Toyama turned around in time to catch Okubo winking at him.

He thought about Okubo's words as he made his way down the narrow hallway toward the sound booth. *...They can hear me in the ready room! I always keep the intercom in there switched off when I'm not using it—I doubt I could've left it on.*

Still, Okubo's remark bothered him. Had someone in the green room overheard him saying something he shouldn't have?

# 6

The feel of the floor under his feet abruptly changed as he went from the green room to the lobby. The hallway to the green room was concrete covered with linoleum: hard and cold. The lobby floor, meanwhile, was covered with a lush carpet.

Tomorrow, opening night, this lobby would be full of audience members. Toyama crossed it and started to climb the spiral staircase to the sound booth. As he did so he heard hushed voices in conversation somewhere. A man's voice, and a woman's—both lowered, as if afraid of being overheard. Toyama halted halfway up the stairs and turned around.

Toyama saw two people standing in a corner by the recessed doors leading into the seating area. A tall man and a slender woman, facing each other. Toyama peered closely at them, with the unmistakable sense that he was watching something he shouldn't. He moved into a position from which they couldn't see him and held his breath.

The man was facing in Toyama's direction but he was half hidden by the wall, so Toyama could only see his face intermittently; the woman's back was turned to him. Toyama saw at once that the man was Shigemori, the director. And though he couldn't see her face, from her clothing and the outlines of her body Toyama knew who the woman was, as well.

"Sadako..." Without realizing it he let slip the name of the woman he loved.

Shigemori had his hands on her shoulders, shaking her gently, and now and then he'd lean close and whisper something into her ear. He certainly didn't appear to be speaking to her as just another actress—the way he drew close to her suggested he wasn't simply giving her pointers on her performance.

Toyama tried—the effort was great, but necessary—to make sure that what he was seeing meant what he thought it did; he was seething. Shigemori was using his position as head of the troupe to hit on a young actress. Toyama found this unforgivable. He could understand it, and he knew that in the theater world it was even tolerated; inexperienced he may have been, but he comprehended that much.

The real question was how Sadako would react. Given her position he knew she couldn't reject Shigemori too forcefully, but he hoped she had enough skill to evade him gently, without injuring his feelings. He knew how hard it would be, but he yearned for her to show him how adroitly she could act here. If she didn't, Toyama would have a hard time trusting the words of love they'd exchanged.

Their relationship was not a physical one, but Sadako had said, "I love you," and Toyama had never doubted it.

Toyama had declared his feelings first. It had been the previous year, during rehearsals for the fall production. The opportunity had presented itself unexpectedly.

The production was a musical involving several dance numbers, and the troupe had invited a pair of professional dancers, both women, to join them as guests. The dancers' schedules were so tight that they often had to miss rehearsal, so Sadako had been drafted as a stand-in. Stand-in was as far as it went, though: she never got to appear onstage.

Toyama had never even imagined Sadako in a dance scene, so when he saw her dancing up close, he was amazed. From the day they'd both taken the troupe's entrance exam she'd stood out; she'd been the object of Toyama's longing attentions ever since then. Even so, he had no way of knowing that her talents included dancing. The first time he saw her move in that provocative way, it further inflamed his passion for her.

But Sadako didn't seem confident in her dancing. Often he would see her hang her head in thought after carrying out some instruction of the choreographer's. Sadako's dancing certainly worked for Toyama, but it didn't seem to satisfy Sadako herself.

Once, during a break, Toyama went to the bathroom. He ran into Sadako next to the communal sink, and he took the opportunity to praise her dancing. "You're pretty good," he said. But she seemed to think he was being sarcastic, and she fixed him with a powerful glare.

"You don't have to use that kind of tone. I'll practice—I'll get better, and then I'll show you."

No doubt the older actresses had been needling her about her dance skills. As a result, she was unable to hear the sincerity in his praise, and so she'd excused herself as an amateur and gotten surly about it to boot.

She turned on her heel to leave. Toyama hurried after her. "I didn't mean it like that at all!"

He placed a hand on her shoulder, but she shook him off, saying, "Look, even I know I'm not any good, okay?"

"Well, I think you are. Please believe me. I'm not being sarcastic or anything: I really think you're good. I was just trying to boost your confidence a little…"

"You're lying."

"I'm not! Look, I'm not the kind of guy to beat around the bush like that. If I thought you were a bad dancer, I'd tell you, honestly."

They stared at each other. Toyama tried to make his pure intentions felt in his gaze.

Maybe it worked. She didn't look entirely convinced, but she managed an awkward smile, nodded, and whispered, "Okay. Thanks."

That was the first time he'd felt a real emotional connection with Sadako.

From then on he tried to give her advice whenever he could, both in secret and openly. If he noticed something while watching her practice, he'd tell her, purely as an objective bystander. He was tireless in his efforts to help her improve as an actress.

Toyama was the kind of guy girls liked, and as Sadako saw the feelings he had for her, she began to open up toward him. She stood out, and as a result she was always having to put up with backbiting and slander from older members of the troupe, vicious rumors and the like. With all that, she was understandably grateful for Toyama's affection.

The interns took turns cleaning the rehearsal space in pairs. One day in September Toyama was paired with Sadako, and they happened to show up at the same time. It was early afternoon, and the space was deserted except for the two of them; they still had well over an hour to themselves before rehearsal was to start.

They saw to the cleaning, including the bathroom, and then Toyama sat down at the piano in the corner of the rehearsal space. It was a broken-down old upright, and several of its strings were out of tune. He contrived to avoid those notes as he set about playing Sadako a few tunes of his own devising.

Sadako stood beside him listening in silence at first, but then she sat down on the bench and let her fingers wander over the keyboard. Not quite a duet, but she did manage to follow along.

She'd never had formal lessons, she told him, but there was one tune she'd learned to play well enough just by watching. It was a mournful melody. Toyama had heard it before, but he couldn't remember what it was called. He stood up as if pushed off the bench; now it was his turn to listen from behind while Sadako played.

Her left hand played the chords with some hesitation, while her right picked out the melody. Her playing wasn't very good, but there was something about it that tugged at Toyama. Not only did she have what it took to shine as an actress, but now it seemed she had a flair for music as well.

He was unable to resist the urge when it came over him. He stared at the white nape of her neck, covered by her long hair; he watched as she lifted her right hand to brush away her bangs and then lowered it again to the keys with a supple movement. Everything about her, everything she did, mingled girlishness and womanliness, and he found it inexpressibly attractive.

Toyama had overheard more than one older member of the troupe describe Sadako as "that creepy girl." The only way Toyama could make sense of it was to figure that Sadako's preternatural beauty struck them—particularly the women—as eerie.

There was no resisting the strength of his feelings toward her, so he gave himself over to them. He hadn't planned on making a pass at her. It was just that his love could no longer be contained.

He moved quite naturally. "Sadako," he said, and embraced her from behind, intending to bring his face close to hers as she gazed down at the keys. But it was as if she had eyes in the back of her head. Sensing his movements, she stood up and caught him in a full-on embrace. He'd been apprehensive, of course, about how he'd be received, afraid of rejection and all the awkwardness and humiliation it would bring. He hadn't dared hope for this kind of acceptance. He'd miscalculated—but in the best possible way.

Toyama was twenty-three, and he'd known his share of women, but never had he experienced greater pleasure than he knew in that hug there in front of the piano. They stood there for a time, cheek-to-cheek, and then they pulled back gently so their lips could find each other. Anyone who happened to be present would have seen something fresh and pure, not lascivious, in their embrace.

Between kisses, they had whispered to each other:

"I've loved you since the moment we first met," Toyama had told her.

And Sadako had responded in kind. "I love you," she'd said.

So what was the meaning of what he saw now? Toyama stamped his feet on the spiral staircase and gnashed his teeth. He wanted to rush in and pull Shige-mori off her. Every time their faces disappeared into the corner he was tormented by a vision of them kissing. But Shigemori, forty-seven this year, was in the prime of his career as an impresario and playwright—a respected name in the theater world. If Toyama made the wrong move things could go badly not just for him but for Sadako as well. He felt as if his chest were being ripped open, but he told himself he'd just have to endure it for now.

As he grew used to the sight of them and began to

calm down a bit, Toyama noticed something strange about Shigemori's expression. He always had an intensity in his gaze when he watched Sadako rehearse, but now he looked like a man possessed. "Possessed": that was the only word for it. He was no longer himself. His cheeks were flushed, his eyes bloodshot, his breathing ragged. From time to time he pressed a hand to his chest.

Watching all this, Toyama started to hope again. It began to appear that Shigemori was making a pass at her, but that Sadako was subtly deflecting his advances. Perhaps she wasn't making herself a liar after all.

Just then, however, she did something unbelievable.

Toyama saw her lean out from the shelter of the corner and press her lips to Shigemori's.

Shigemori pulled back, as if startled, and stared at her wide-eyed. It seemed that Sadako had done something Shigemori had neither expected nor desired.

Toyama knew that his own expression of astonishment must match Shigemori's. His own eyes were wide as he watched Sadako from behind.

But she didn't stop there. She pulled back a little, and then reached her left hand out toward Shigemori's crotch while Shigemori watched in surprise. She brought her palm up next to where his testicles must be and pretended to cup them from beneath. Then she actually squeezed them two or three times, as if playing with rubber balls.

Shigemori pulled back, his face clouded over with confusion; he grimaced, as if about to burst into tears...

Shigemori began to collapse—fainting? He staggered and leaned back against the wall, chest heaving, one hand pressed to his chest and the other rubbing his neck.

*What's going on?*

Just a moment ago Toyama had hated Shigemori, but now he found himself sympathizing with the man. Right about now they were both equally confused. Neither could assign meaning to Sadako's actions. Why had she suddenly kissed Shigemori? Why had she cradled his testicles in her hand? She had to mean something by it.

Sadako stepped away from the wall, leaving Shigemori there in his altered physical state, and suddenly turned toward Toyama. It was as if she'd known he was there all along. About twenty yards separated them, and he was mostly hidden behind the railing of the staircase, but still she looked straight at him, as if the eyes in the back of her head had already located him. It reminded him of how she'd reacted when he'd tried to embrace her that day when she was playing the piano. The way she'd moved, then and now, was amazing—intuition didn't begin to cover it.

Sadako met Toyama's gaze and flashed him a victorious wink.

*You know what's going on, don't you?* said her look. But he didn't.

Sadako disappeared into the hallway leading to the green room, leaving confusion in her wake.

In contrast to Sadako's resolute, purposeful gaze, Shigemori appeared to be seeing nothing, his hollow gaze still turned toward the ceiling. He hadn't noticed Toyama in front of him. Sadako had disappeared speedily, leaving him sluggish, bereft of his usually scintillating wits.

At length he seemed to come around. He pushed open the door and staggered into the theater. He was a tall, slender man, but at the moment his limbs looked leaden.

Both Sadako and Shigemori having left his field of vision, Toyama went into the sound booth.

His tapes were all ready. The curtain could go up any time, and he'd have no problems.

Finally Shigemori's voice came over the intercom.

"Okay, everyone. We're about to start the second act."

His voice quavered enough to be noticeable even to someone who hadn't just witnessed what Toyama had.

# 7

The curtain had gone up on the dress rehearsal's second act, but Toyama couldn't concentrate on his job. The scene he'd just seen kept flickering before his mind's eye, making him careless about checking for stray sounds on the tape. Jealousy, rage, and shock welled up from the depths of his heart and turned into a rushing current that threatened to engulf him.

For six months now, he'd considered his and Sadako's relationship to be that of lovers. When nobody was watching they'd hold and kiss each other, but that and honeyed words marked the extent of their relationship: no matter how he sought it, nothing more was forthcoming. Still, he was satisfied with what they had. He decided that it must be her youth—she was only eighteen—that kept things from developing physically. He found her innocence pleasing, in a way. She was a virgin. Of that he'd never had a doubt.

The only thing that nagged at him was Sadako's extreme caution that nobody else find out about their relationship. It seemed a bit excessive to Toyama.

When they were alone, her attitude proclaimed that she truly loved him. But when they were with other members of the troupe, she treated him with particular coldness, so that he was wracked with anxiety. For his part, he always looked on her as someone special to him, no matter where they were. But not her: when people were around, she treated him like just another face in the crowd.

His fondest wish was for her to sit by him, even in the presence of their colleagues, and simply look at him. He was tired of being ignored in front of the others: it only made him watch her more closely, only increased his desire to elude the others so he could hold and kiss her.

He could understand her not wanting to be gossiped about, but still, he wished things would change. When he told her this, however, she always gave him the same answer.

*I don't want to let everybody know how close we are. What we have is our little secret, and I want you to keep it that way. Okay? You can't tell anybody about us. Promise me—if you don't, I'll lose you.*

Her explanation never convinced him. Why did things have to be kept so secret? What he'd witnessed her doing with Shigemori just now suggested a possible reason.

Everybody who joined the troupe did so because they wanted to make it as an actor or actress. Sadako radiated that desire even more strongly than most, and with her it was mingled with something in her gaze that challenged society in ways that normal people couldn't quite fathom. It verged on hostility. Sometimes Toyama saw a coldness and contempt for the world in her eyes that made him flinch.

*The world doesn't hate you as much as you think it does.* He tried again and again to tell her that, but she never listened. She'd just scold him for being naïve, saying if he went through life like that, they'd get him—at times like that she acted like a much older woman.

He wondered what there was in her past to make her that way, and sometimes he even tried to ask, nonchalantly. But she always evaded his questions, and so he was never able to grasp the true nature of her near-enmity toward society.

The only way for Sadako to triumph over the world was to become a famous actress. It was the one thing an eighteen-year-old girl could do that would command universal admiration in one fell swoop. He was sure she knew that.

Which led Toyama to a deduction. Becoming a star meant grabbing every chance that presented itself. What could she do right here, right now? The answer was plain. She could cozy up to Shigemori, who held absolute power over the troupe, in hopes of getting a part. That had to be how she'd gotten such an important role in the current production. It was, after all, a major coup for an intern who'd only been with the troupe for a year.

*But how?* Toyama didn't want to think about that. The image of the two of them in the corner kept returning to his thoughts, tormenting him.

He thought he knew now why she'd wanted to keep her relationship with him so secret. It was quite clear. If it became common knowledge in the troupe that she and

Toyama were lovers, word of it would naturally reach Shigemori. Certainly Shigemori would not be pleased to learn she had a boyfriend, and that would lessen her chances of ingratiating herself with him.

*Am I just being toyed with? By this nineteen-year-old woman-child? This sylph?*

Toyama hung his head—still wearing his headphones. For a moment, his eyes left the stage.

The stage manager's voice crackled over the intercom. "Hey, Toyama, you forgot the ring!"

He looked up. He'd missed his timing. Hurriedly he pressed the play button and the sound of a ringing telephone issued forth. It was late, so the actor onstage had been forced to ad lib; now he waited for it to ring twice before picking up the receiver. As he did so, Toyama stopped the tape.

Disaster had been averted, but all the same the stage manager berated him. "Idiot! Are you even watching the stage?"

"Sorry," Toyama said immediately.

"Just pay attention, alright?"

"I will."

He sighed as he broke out in a cold sweat. He had no excuse. He'd lost himself, lost his concentration, and caused problems for his colleagues. All because of his love for Sadako.

*Shit. Get a hold of yourself.*

He couldn't stand not being able to control his feelings. He'd always thought of himself as strong-willed, not at all the type to let himself be swept along by his emotions. And look at him now—all on account of a woman.

He shook his head, trying to clear it of lewd fantasies. It was no use. Onstage, Sadako's scene was starting.

The Girl in Black appeared from stage left and stood wordlessly behind a middle-aged man who was yelling into a telephone. The man sensed something behind him, fell silent, and turned around. The stage went dark for an instant. When the lights came on again, the Girl in Black had disappeared. It was a remarkable effect, really, a skillful combination of lighting and set design.

The man dropped the receiver, terrified: he'd just seen a girl's ghost...

The scene was pivotal, the key to understanding the play as a whole.

The Girl in Black had only been onstage for a moment before she disappeared. Toyama called out to her.

"Sadako..."

It was less a cry than a plea that she return, that shadow he'd only just glimpsed. Suddenly he had a premonition that she would disappear from his life just like she had from the stage.

*Hey, now, don't go borrowing trouble.*

He kept his eyes on the stage. The Girl in Black had one more scene.

This time she appeared from the rear center of the stage. She stood on a platform stage center and opened her mouth as if to speak. But then the lights went out again. A complete change of scene. In the end the audience would never know what the Girl in Black was trying to say. That was how it was set up.

Toyama was projecting his own feelings onto the events onstage. When she opened her mouth he didn't want her to stop, he wanted her to say it loud. Stop hiding it from the other members of the troupe—let everyone know about their relationship.

*Toyama, I love you.*

How wonderful it would be to hear her say that in front of a huge audience. Once everybody knew, they wouldn't have to embrace in secret anymore. What a relief that would be.

He wanted to be able to speak his love for Sadako openly, fearing no one. He'd make doubly sure Shigemori heard about it, to let him know that it was him, not Shigemori, that Sadako loved. Then even Shigemori couldn't persist in the kind of acts Toyama had just witnessed.

He'd gotten confused. It was Sadako who'd taken such an active role in what he'd seen in the empty lobby—not Shigemori.

The Girl in Black disappeared from the stage, leaving only an afterimage—it was quite effective, really, the way she made such a deep impression in spite of her minimal time onstage. She said nothing that wasn't necessary—certainly not goodbye.

But he didn't want her to disappear like that in real life.

# 8

The dress rehearsal ended without a long feedback session, just a "Good job, everyone."

When Shigemori said that, it meant that everyone could go home. They were free. Toyama was tired. He put a hand on his chest in relief. He'd made mistakes, and if the director had started to complain about them there'd be no end to it.

They weren't getting to go home early because the run-through had been especially good, though; apparently Shigemori himself was so tired that he just had to let them go. The cast and crew stood around on the stage or in the aisles and Shigemori said a brief word to each of them about their performances that night, telling them all to give it their best over the next three weeks. He was pale, and slumped down into a seat; he made no move to stand.

The actors, on the other hand, were glowing with elation: opening day was tomorrow. They all congratulated each other on a job well done, and then began to drift apart, some to go home and some to rehearse more. The theater itself closed at midnight, so they all had to be out by then. There was a night watchman who checked to make sure none of them hung around later than that.

Toyama headed back to the sound booth to clean up. "Well, then," he muttered as he tried to decide if there was anything left to do for tomorrow.

His mind was still occupied with Sadako and his conflicting feelings toward her, but he'd managed to check all his tapes over the course of the run-through, and nothing was out of order. He trusted his ears. No matter how scattered his thoughts, his ears would have picked up any noise that was out of place. Anything he might have missed on his headphones would be too soft for the audience to detect, and definitely too soft to disrupt the performance.

*The cassette recorder—I almost forgot.*

From a shelf beneath the desk he took out a cassette deck. It had leather straps on the sides to make it easier to carry: now he pulled it out by one of those straps.

It was the newest model, made so you could slip a strap over a shoulder and carry it around, and it had a built-in microphone. It was good for recording things like street noise: he could take this outside and record with it, and then transfer the recording to a reel-to-reel tape for editing.

The tape in this deck, he realized, did contain things he'd rather nobody hear. Yesterday afternoon, when the interns were alone in their rehearsal space, they'd gotten up to a little mischief.

Okubo had instigated the whole thing. He was particularly good at impressions, or so he said, and he'd announced that he wanted to record some so he could evaluate himself. This model of cassette deck was still not very common, so he asked Toyama how to operate it, as he gathered everyone around.

Okubo began running through a few of his best bits for the small crowd, which consisted entirely of interns. After each ovation, Okubo rewound the tape and played it back, cracking up over his own performance as he reviewed it. The reviews themselves were amusing, and the tape-deck-centered revelry escalated.

At first Okubo was doing impressions of TV personalities, but after a while he shifted his target to people they knew. One of the leading actors in the troupe had a peculiar way of speaking, so he poked fun at that, and everyone laughed. Finally he set his sights on Shigemori. This was forbidden territory. Some of the more timid interns went to the office to make doubly sure Shigemori wasn't in—there would be hell to pay if they were overheard. Once they had ascertained that he was out, Okubo cut loose with his most energetic and elaborate impression yet.

Okubo had Shigemori down pat, from the tone he took when giving feedback to the overwrought voice he'd use when bawling someone out for a bad performance to the lines he'd use to seduce new actresses. They all knew Shigemori well enough to find the performance hilarious, and Okubo went on and on, the tape recorder on all the while.

Toyama had gotten it all on tape—the very tape before him now. What he needed to do was to have a blank tape all set in the deck so it would be ready if he needed it during the premiere or later. But he didn't have another tape. He wracked his brain for a solution.

This tape, with everyone laughing at Shigemori, was a dangerous object. If the director happened to hear it, he wouldn't let them off with just a yelling-at. The listeners would have it bad enough, but there was no telling what he'd do to Okubo for mimicking him trying to pick up a woman—and failing, at that.

Toyama elected to erase the tape.

To do that, all he had to do was press record with the microphone turned off. The tape would be restored to its original blank state. It was too much trouble to figure out what was where on the tape, so he decided just to erase the whole thing, start to finish. The problem was, that would take forty-five minutes.

He pressed the record button and watched as the tape began to advance. This would destroy all evidence of their little game.

With nothing else to do, he glanced idly at the stage, where a few actors were walking around, checking their marks. Sadako was standing on the dais at stage center.

She had her mouth open as if about to speak: they were rehearsing the bit where the lights went out. Over and over, until she was satisfied. What was it she was trying to say? No, the question should be, did Shigemori even have any lines in mind for her when he wrote the scene? If so, Toyama knew he wanted to hear them directly from Sadako.

He leaned close to the glass and focused on Sadako.

She seemed to be aware that he was watching her: she stopped, lowered her hands, and turned her gaze in his direction. He could feel it, even at that distance. At that moment, they were connected by the thread of their mutual gaze.

The overhead light was on in the sound booth, so no doubt Toyama's face was visible from the other side of the glass. Meanwhile, the lights were on over the stage, giving it a totally different ambience from the dress rehearsal: Sadako's face looked different under the white light, her color contrasting with her black costume, but differently than usual. There was something obscene about it, as if her underclothes were showing through.

Sadako stepped down from the stage into the seats, heading for the lobby.

*She's coming up to the booth.*

He imagined her movements. Now she was crossing the lobby; now she was climbing the spiral staircase to the sound booth. She was in no hurry—in fact, she was taking her time, to make him anxious. She moved with light elegance.

He waited for the knock at the door.

*...3, 2, 1, 0.*

At zero, the door swung open, without a knock.

Sadako slipped into the room and closed the door behind her.

"Did you call?" She was quite alluring in her stage clothes, up close.

Toyama remained silent and unsmiling. He hoped that his anger was showing through in his expression, but he had no idea what he really looked like to her. In any case, he was trying to look as out-of-sorts as he could, but Sadako just ignored it and crossed the room. She unfolded a metal chair and sat down on it.

Toyama maintained his silence. Finally Sadako spoke, pretending to have noticed just now. "Hey, what are you so mad about?"

Of course she knew why he was angry: she had to know. It annoyed him that she was pretending not to, and he snapped.

"What the hell was that back there?"

Sadako raised an eyebrow. "Oh, that." She pursed her lips and laughed mischievously.

"Did you know I was watching when you did that to Mr. Shigemori?" They always called him *Mister* Shigemori, so Toyama called him that now, out of habit, but it didn't match his mood, so he made a show of muttering, "Shigemori, that bastard."

"Are you jealous?"

She was sitting on the edge of her seat, and now she put both hands on the chair and made a little move as if to get up.

"Jealous? I'm concerned for you, baby."

It was a lie, and a transparent one at that. He wasn't concerned for anyone but himself. All his rage sprang from a heart tortured by jealousy.

"Toyama, maybe you'd better not call me 'baby'."

Her tone was not harsh, but it was firm. Toyama was somewhat taken aback by this display of will on her part, and he had to bite his lip to keep from saying, "I'm sorry."

"No matter how much you cozy up to Shigemori, I just don't think it's going to help you in the future. If you have a dream you've got to reach out and take it on your own."

*Reach out and take it...* What a cliché—Toyama was disgusted with himself for uttering something straight out of a teen soap opera.

"A dream? Toyama, do you know what my dream is?"

"To become a great actress, right?"

Sadako brought a hand to one cheek and gave a hard-to-define smile.

"How many people do you think would come see me if I made it as a stage actress?"

"You don't have to stick to the stage. There's TV, movies."

"What about that, that red light—see it?"

Sadako pointed to the cassette deck that was erasing Okubo's impressions. A tiny lamp glowed red, signifying that it was recording.

"The cassette deck?"

"It's so much smaller than a reel-to-reel. Looks really easy to record on, too."

"Yes, it is pretty convenient."

"I wonder if images will be like that, too. If we'll ever be able to record images, not just on film like in a movie theater, but on something small like a cassette tape."

What she was saying didn't sound all that far-fetched—no doubt that day was fast approaching.

"I'm sure we will, sooner or later. Maybe someday we'll be able to sit at home and watch one of your movies on TV."

"But that's a long way off, isn't it?" She sounded depressed about it.

"It's not impossible, though. You could do it."

"But it would be too late."

"What do you mean?"

"By that time, I'd be an old woman."

She had a point. Even assuming Sadako kept steadily maturing as an actress, by the time a cassette-like image-storage system came into widespread use, she'd no longer be considered young.

"Don't be in such a rush."

"I don't want to get old. I want to stay young for-ever. Wouldn't that be great?"

Nobody fears aging like an aspiring young actress, reflected Toyama. Sadako was evidently no exception.

"I wouldn't mind growing old with you."

It was almost a proposal, despite the casual way he said it. And he meant it. Aging held no horrors for him, as long as he and Sadako could live together. And when he finally died of old age, he could do it with a smile on his face provided she was there beside him. For an instant Toyama imagined dying in Sadako's arms. She was gazing into his eyes while the world receded spinning into the distance. He was old...but for some reason Sadako was still her present age. In his head the image was startlingly clear.

The muscles around Sadako's mouth relaxed as she realized that Toyama really did want to be with her. She knit her brow and said, a little defensively, "You're under the impression that I like Mr. Shigemori, aren't you? You've got the wrong idea."

"Well, I don't want to think that. But considering what I saw you do—"

She wouldn't let him finish. She shook her head and said, "No, no. You misunderstand. I can't stand him. He comes on way too strong. In fact, he scares me. It's like he's obsessed with me—he's just creepy. I hate it. Why can't he be a little more laid back—especially at his age?"

So even Shigemori had struck out with Sadako. Toyama actually began to feel a little sorry for him—was it possible that he was seriously in love with Sadako, at age forty-seven?

"To be honest, it's really hard for me—I don't know how to tell you what I really feel. I want to believe you, Sadako, but..."

Sadako leaned forward in the folding chair and put a hand on Toyama's knee.

"Toyama," she said.

She was only nineteen, but it seemed she knew just how to relieve the frustration of a man suffering from jealousy.

She stood up and turned off the lights. Once she'd turned out the desk light, the booth was dark except for what light found its way through the window from the stage below. It was enough to dimly illuminate Sadako's body. But then the last actors left the stage, and that light too was extinguished. All was black except for the tiny red glow of the record light on the cassette deck in the corner.

Something clicked in the darkness. Sadako must have locked the door from the inside. After a while, Toyama felt her weight on his knees. So slender to look at, she was surprisingly heavy.

He could see nothing: only by her weight did he know she was there. She guided his hands as he undressed her. They unzipped her dress in the back, and then she slipped it off over her head. Now Sadako was straddling him in her underwear as he sat there.

At the soft touch of her skin, the outlines of Sadako's body took shape in Toyama's mind. She'd taken off her dress, but ironically she was now becoming the Girl in Black herself. The fact that he couldn't see her in the darkness only stimulated his imagination as her naked form took on solidity in his mind's eye. The red glow from the tape deck only made her blacker.

As he savored the satisfaction of having her all to

himself at last, Toyama's frustration and jealousy melted away.

He lost track of time. He forgot himself completely as they touched each other's bodies, as he stroked her hair, as he lifted her head and ran his lips over her neck; naturally, his desire progressed to the next level. But every time he started to reach a hand between her legs, she would stop his hand—sometimes gently, and sometimes brusquely. Finally, as if to distract him, she reached into his shorts.

It took him no time at all to climax: her hands moved, and in response Toyama finished, stifling a moan.

Not a drop of his ejaculate hit his clothes or the floor: Sadako caught it all in her hands. In his abandon, Toyama was unable to figure out what she was doing now. From the sounds, he thought she might be rubbing her hands together in it. Once she'd covered her hands in his fluid like lather from a bar of soap, she put her arms around his face, his neck, and embraced him. He smelled his own.

Then Sadako whispered in his ear, barely loud enough to hear, "Don't ever love me more than you do now. I don't want to lose you, Toyama."

It didn't feel as if she'd said the words at all, but rather as if they'd been delivered straight into his brain.

*Toyama, I love you.*

Was he hallucinating from the strength of his desire? No—her voice pressed itself directly into his mind.

These were the words he wanted everyone to hear—
if indeed he was hearing them himself. He especially
wanted Shigemori to hear them.

"Sadako," he whispered, in a dry, scratchy voice,
"you'd make me so happy if you'd just say you love me
in front of everyone..."

But she shook her head.

At that moment his foot hit the cabinet. He heard
something fall. He'd forgotten himself in his love for
Sadako, but just for an instant his attention was claimed
by the altar hidden at his feet, and the offering lain in
front of it.

*Toyama, I love you.*

Again, her voice coming into his brain—and together with it he thought he heard, from somewhere, the
sound of a baby crying. It wasn't his imagination: he definitely heard a newborn baby crying, behind Sadako.

# 9

*November 1990*

Every cell in his body was reliving the touch of Sadako's skin. This wasn't like a mental recollection: it felt as if the memory were engraved in his very DNA.

He told Yoshino about that episode from his youth, but he didn't go into every single little detail. He just gave him the general outlines, the salient points of the day of the final dress rehearsal. But as he spoke he was remembering Sadako's voice, the softness of her skin, the feel of her hair, as if it were yesterday.

*Toyama, I love you.*

Her voice still lingered in his ear—whether he'd really heard it or only hallucinated it, he could recreate its resonance, its mysterious ambience, exactly. It was the voice of the only woman he'd ever met with whom he could have been truly happy.

He wanted to see her again, if at all possible. Where was she now? What was she doing? The fact that Yoshino couldn't find her was at least proof that she hadn't made a name for herself as an actress. That in itself he found unbelievable, for a woman with such a unique allure as hers. He began to feel uneasy.

He found it took courage just to ask. But somehow he managed to voice his query. "By the way, Mr. Yoshino. What do you think Sadako's doing now? Please, don't keep anything back from me—whatever you might know."

Yoshino rested his chin on his hand; he licked the cover of his fountain pen with the tip of his tongue.

"Of all the ridiculous... I'm trying to find out what happened to her. How could I have any idea what she's doing now?"

"I think you people know something. Don't you think it's a bit unfair for you to ask me all these questions and then not answer mine?"

"But..."

Toyama leaned forward earnestly and looked Yoshino square in his bearded face.

"Is Sadako alive?"

He had to come straight out and ask it: otherwise they'd keep going in circles.

Yoshino looked taken aback by Toyama's seriousness. He made a strange face, then shook his head twice, gently.

"I hate to say it, but she's probably..." Warning him that nothing was definite yet, Yoshino told Toyama that the information his colleague Asakawa had come across gave them reason to speculate that Sadako Yamamura was no longer alive. There was a possibility that she'd been involved in some kind of incident, and that it had happened right after her disappearance from the troupe

121

twenty-four years ago. Again, it was still only specula-
tion. But…

But it was enough. It was the development Toyama
had feared, and it didn't surprise him. He'd had a feeling,
for he didn't know how long now, that Sadako was no
longer of this world.

Still, hearing Yoshino state it as a near-certainty
caused a physical reaction in Toyama that was far more
honest than he'd expected. To his surprise, tears began
not just rolling down his cheeks, but actually falling to
splash on the floor. In his forty-seven years he'd never
dreamed his body was capable of such a thing. She was
the one burning love of his life… But that was twenty-
four years ago. He was more experienced now—he knew
he was even something of a playboy—and now he was
weeping over confirmation of Sadako's death. He
couldn't help but see something comical in it.

Startled, Yoshino searched in his satchel until he
found a tissue. Wordlessly he offered it to Toyama.

"Sorry, I don't know what…" Toyama trailed off and
blew his nose.

"I know how you must be feeling."

But Yoshino's words sounded utterly fake. *How
could you know?*

Toyama started to blow his nose again, but then decided to ask something that had been on his mind all
along.

"By the way, you said you'd talked on the phone
with some of my old colleagues from the troupe."

"Yes. Iino, Kitajima, and Kato."

"And that they all knew I had a relationship with Sadako."

"That's right."

That didn't sit right with Toyama, given the excessive care Sadako had taken to ensure that their relationship wasn't made public. Toyama, too, in response to her demands, had made a point of not mentioning it to anybody. In spite of all that, they knew. He wondered how.

"I don't get it. I was pretty sure we'd kept it under wraps."

Seeing that Toyama had gotten his emotions under control, Yoshino ventured a smile.

"You were fooling yourself, my friend. When two people are in love, people notice, no matter how much they try to hide it."

"Did they say anything specific?"

Yoshino gave a little half-laugh, half-sigh. "Oh, maybe you didn't know about this. Well, it seems someone played a trick on you."

"A trick?"

"This is twenty-four years ago we're talking about, after all, so it seemed pointless to me at first, but hearing what you had to say has cleared something up for me. Things make sense now."

Yoshino then told Toyama something he'd heard from Kitajima. Not precisely as Kitajima had told him— he blended what he'd gotten from Kitajima with what he'd just learned from Toyama to come up with his own version of what had happened.

It was an April afternoon, the closing day of their three-week run.

It was closing day, and the interns were all gathered in the big room behind the dressing rooms, enjoying a rare moment of leisure. After that day's performance, a late matinee, the play would be over: they'd break down the sets and lighting, and then the wrap party would begin. A week or more's vacation awaited them after that. For the first time in three months, they'd be able to really relax.

Already feeling somewhat liberated, Okubo had gathered everybody to watch him do impressions again. Kitajima was still among them at this point, cheering him on with the rest.

It wasn't clear who had brought it up. Once Okubo was all revved up, though, somebody mentioned the tape they'd recorded him on last time. This brought back memories: oh, that's right—we sure had fun that time, etc. etc. Meanwhile Okubo lost interest in his impressions and started gathering wool. Then he suddenly started to worry about that cassette, asking everybody what had happened to it. Nobody knew. Finally he realized if anybody would know, it was Toyama, he being in charge of the tape deck.

That tape constituted a grave danger to Okubo. If Shigemori found it, then at the very least his week's vacation might be canceled. He decided that he wouldn't be able to make it through closing day with any peace of mind unless he disposed of the tape.

So he said he was going up to the sound booth to look for it. As Okubo lost interest in his impressions in order to concentrate on finding the tape, Kitajima lost interest in Okubo. He left the room, heading for the restroom off the lobby. Before the doors to the theater opened, that restroom was usually empty, and Kitajima always went there when he needed to sit down to do his business.

He walked together with Okubo as far as the lobby, then they separated, Okubo climbing the spiral stairs to the sound booth and Kitajima going into the empty restroom.

He took his time. When he was finished he made a call from the pay phone to check on some tickets, and when he finally returned to the big room he almost ran into a red-faced Shigemori rushing from the room. At that moment Kitajima sensed that something bad had happened, but since Shigemori didn't seem to notice him at all he decided that he wasn't the target of the director's anger, and so he relaxed.

In terms of timing, it seemed likely that Shigemori had learned of the cassette and was overreacting to it. But as Kitajima watched to see what Shigemori would do next, he saw something unexpected.

Shigemori was definitely flustered, but Kitajima couldn't tell if he was angry or disturbed. He opened the door of the women's dressing room and called for Sadako

Yamamura repeatedly, in a low voice.

Kitajima watched from behind the sink. A woman came to the door in response to Shigemori's call. Probably Sadako, but since she didn't step into the hallway where Shigemori stood, Kitajima couldn't see her at all. From what Shigemori said next, though, it was clear who it was.

"I don't believe you, Sadako."

Shigemori seemed to have a hand on her shoulder, now shaking her, now stroking her, now with a pleading look on his face, now with a threatening scowl, but looking straight at her all the while. Sometimes his eyes seemed to brim with tears. In profile, as Kitajima saw him, Shigemori was showing commingled love and hatred.

Shigemori harangued Sadako like that for a good ten minutes. After he released her, she didn't come out again until it was almost show time. When she finally emerged in order to prepare her costume and props, her expression was one that Kitajima told Yoshino he'd never forgotten to this day.

Deep despair. He couldn't think of how else to describe it. She'd been thrust into this, her first role, at the last minute, and audiences hadn't reacted well to her. As the run dragged on she'd gotten progressively more depressed. That might have been part of it now. In any case, she looked like she'd hit rock bottom. Usually she emanated a kind of aura, but now all the light had gone out of her. She looked utterly enervated. Kitajima watched from behind as she climbed the stairs to the backstage area; she seemed to be filled with an inexpressible pain.

That was all Kitajima saw that day.

He only found out what had really happened several years later, after he'd quit the troupe and joined an event-planning company.

He and Okubo had gotten together for a drink—their first meeting after quitting the troupe and going their own ways. Kitajima had mentioned that final afternoon before the last performance. "What happened that day, anyway?"

Yoshino's subsequent narrative was based on what Kitajima had repeated to him of Okubo's reply.

Okubo had gone up to the sound booth to look for the tape containing his imitation of Shigemori. Toyama wasn't there, so he made use of his absence to ransack the room. He found the cassette deck under the desk with the tape still in it. He listened to it from the beginning. From the label, he knew this was the tape he was after, but on playback he couldn't find the impressions. He fast-forwarded and then pressed play again, repeating this over and over until he was satisfied he hadn't missed it, finally concluding that "somebody must've erased it already." Then, just as he began to relax, his ears began to pick up a woman's moan.

"Ahhh... ohhh..." was what he heard, along with some ragged breathing. Okubo was still a virgin, so he didn't know what he was hearing at first. He kept listening out of sheer curiosity, until gradually the moaning turned into words. It was then he realized who the voice belonged to.

"Sadako…" muttered Okubo. That was her voice, he was sure of it. That was her, panting, moaning, and calling out a name, saying she loved someone.

*Don't ever love me more than you do now. I don't want to lose you, Toyama.*

The breathing was forced and now and then it stopped; the voice was excited.

*Toyama, I love you.*

Okubo was enraptured. Forget about the words, the voice alone had something about it that would stimulate any listener's sensitivities.

But something abruptly brought Okubo back to his senses. The words arrived in his mind with all their meaning, and when they did, his body was invaded by an uncontrollable emotion. He couldn't put a name on it. It involved a strong desire for Sadako. He'd liked Sadako too, just like Toyama, and his feelings had been decidedly mixed as he'd watched the way things developed from rehearsals on through the actual performances.

Maybe he just couldn't stand watching the girl he loved, this girl younger than him, cozy up to the director to get a part. Maybe at heart he was a sore loser who hated seeing the girl he loved make her stage debut before him. Judging by this tape, she loved Toyama: maybe he was just burning with jealousy toward him. And on top of all that, it might have been pure malice that had

made him think of presenting this as evidence to Shigemori, who was openly trying to seduce Sadako.

*You old bastard, it's just like I've always thought
when I was doing impressions of you: the jilted-lover
role suits you.*

Okubo felt his face grow hot as he contemplated all
these factors. But the only explanation he had for what
he did next was that the devil had made him do it.

He rewound the tape a bit, hit play, and turned up
the volume. Making sure that Sadako could be heard, he
then turned on the intercom to the green room and
dressing rooms. Everybody would be able to hear Sadako
calling Toyama's name ecstatically.

At this point, Toyama gave a cry, almost a scream.
"Holy…"

Yoshino gave him a sympathetic look. "You really
didn't know?"

He'd never even suspected. "How could I have
known? I was gone. A friend of mine had come to see the
play, and we'd gone out to lunch." Lunch was provided
in the theater for everybody, but on that day of all days,
Toyama had been invited to eat out.

"Everybody was told to keep quiet about it."

"By whom?"

"Shigemori, of course."

"Shigemori heard the tape?"

"It would seem so. It so happened he was in the
green room at the time. When Sadako's voice came over

the intercom, he heard it. That's why he rushed to Sadako all in a tizzy like that."

Both Yoshino and Toyama knew what had happened to Shigemori after that.

The last performance went off without a hitch. They cleaned up the stage, and then had the wrap party as scheduled. Once that was finished Shigemori had collected the other troupe leaders for a game of mah-jongg, as was his wont. According to Yoshino's information, at that time one of the leading actors, Arima, had recounted to Shigemori an example of Sadako's peculiar powers. This in turn prompted Shigemori to get excited and say, "I'm going to storm her room."

He was unusually drunk, and no one could restrain him by word or action. His companions decided that it would be dangerous for him physically if he drank any more; everybody gave up on mah-jongg and began to get ready to go home. But nobody (they said) expected Shigemori to actually go through with it.

What really happened would remain forever enshrouded in darkness. Not a soul knew if Shigemori's passions had really driven him to visit Sadako's place in the middle of the night. Shigemori did show up at the rehearsal space the next day, but he was so quiet as to be almost unrecognizable. He just wandered around aimlessly, doing nothing in particular, and then he sat down in a chair and stopped breathing, as if going to sleep. The cause of death was determined to be sudden heart failure. Everyone assumed that the impossible performance schedule had hastened his death, and nobody was particularly surprised.

There was something ironic in the story, Toyama felt. He thought of all the agonizing days he'd spent in the sound booth back then, all the jealousy he'd suffered, despite Sadako's assurances that she loved him, because of her insistence on keeping things secret from Shigemori. He'd always thought how wonderful it would be if everyone could hear the sincerity in her voice when she said she loved him. Ironically, they had. He'd wished that Shigemori in particular could hear it, as a reproof for the way he was using his authority to hit on Sadako. In fact, he had.

Toyama hung his head as he thought about it. He'd told Sadako, straight out, his heart's secret desire.

*...Sadako...you'd make me so happy if you'd just say you love me in front of everyone...*

The tape had been broadcast from the sound booth. Toyama himself was master of the sound booth. At the time, he'd been out to lunch, but Sadako probably didn't know that. Knowing what he most wanted, Sadako had no doubt concluded that she knew who had played her moans over the intercom.

There was no sense stamping his feet about it now. He didn't know what had happened with Shigemori that night, but it was all but certain that Sadako's disappearance was connected to her relationship with Toyama. She probably felt he'd betrayed her. Nothing could be more of an affront to a young woman than what she thought he'd done to her: betrayed her and played her sex-cries over a loudspeaker.

And so she'd quit the troupe, and left Toyama without a word.

He felt drained of all strength. Sadako was probably dead. He couldn't explain himself to her. It was too late for regrets. It was all over, everything. But Okubo's mischief was in a perverse way just what Toyama had wanted. He didn't know how to feel about it.

He recalled little Okubo's face. For the first time in a long time, he realized he wanted to see Okubo. To see him, and to find out in greater detail what had happened.

But Toyama himself had quit Theater Group Soaring two months after Sadako had left, and he'd lost touch with his former colleagues.

"By the way, you wouldn't know how I could get in touch with Okubo, would you?"

Yoshino, as a reporter, seemed like he might have better information than Toyama about things like that. After all, he'd tracked down all eight former interns.

"Okubo is...well, he's dead."

"Dead?"

Taken by surprise, Toyama jerked backward. Something felt wrong.

"I was only able to make contact with four of you, yourself included."

"What about the other four?"

"Don't you see? They're all dead."

Toyama and Okubo were the oldest of their group;

Toyama was forty-seven, the same age Okubo would have been if he'd lived. The same age Shigemori had been when he died. Most of the others were two or three years younger—too young to die, at any rate. What were the chances of four out of eight of them being dead by their mid-forties? Not great, Toyama figured.

"How did Okubo die?" It had to be either an illness or an accident.

"I know it happened ten years ago. I don't know how. Why don't you ask Mr. Kitajima? He's my source."

Toyama decided he'd do that. Of course he would. "Do you know how I can get in touch with him?"

Yoshino searched his briefcase, pulled out his notepad, and read off the phone number. It was in the city. As he copied it down, Toyama thought he'd try Kitajima the very next day.

## 10

Toyama left the subway station and headed down Hitotsugi Street toward his office. He felt cold sweat trickle down his back, rivulet after rivulet. The weather was balmy, considering it was almost December. Gazing at the cloudless sky should have given Toyama a corresponding sense of peace, but it didn't.

Yesterday he'd contacted Kitajima for the first time in ages. The things they'd talked about—he couldn't get them out of his head now. They left a bad aftertaste, one that he couldn't quite define, and couldn't get rid of.

According to Kitajima, Okubo and the other three had all died within the last few years, one after the other. And in each case the cause of death had been heart-related: angina pectoris, myocardial infarction, heart failure. But there was another, even scarier, coincidence.

When Okubo had played the tape of Sadako in bliss over the intercom into the big room, three interns had been present: Shinichiro Mori, Keiko Takahata, and Mayu Yumi. Those three plus Shigemori, who'd also happened to be there, made four. And it so happened that all four had died of heart-related illnesses. They'd died at different times—Shigemori the very next day, the other three only twenty-odd years later—but still, it was

134

too much to be dismissed as mere coincidence.

The first of the three to die was Okubo, the main culprit: he'd gone at age thirty-seven from a myocardial infarction. But in any case, all five of the people who had heard the tape were dead. It was disturbing, to say the least.

*Did I hear it?*

Toyama began to worry. He hadn't actually listened to the tape, but he'd heard what was on it—that is, he'd received Sadako's voice directly into his brain, where it had resonated as if to engrave itself there. Those words of hers that had once brought him unmatched ecstasy now began to take on a different meaning.

He realized there was something he'd forgotten to tell Yoshino the other day. Which was that he was absolutely sure there was no way Sadako's voice could have been recorded on that tape.

Even now, twenty-four years later, he could remember it clearly. In order to erase Okubo's impressions he had pressed the record button on the tape deck. Normally this would record over what was already on the tape, but in this case he wanted simply to make the tape blank, so he turned off the built-in microphone. This was important—he'd checked several times to make sure it was off. He had a visual memory of it: the VU meter that measured the recording level didn't budge from zero.

Which meant—it was the logical conclusion—that Sadako's voice could not have been recorded on that tape.

Suddenly he felt dizzy—he staggered down the sidewalk, then leaned up against a telephone pole. The dizziness and shortness of breath were particularly bad today. Usually if he rested for a few minutes his spells would pass, but now the dizziness got so bad he felt like throwing up. He didn't feel like this was going to go away anytime soon.

He entered the building where he worked. His department was on the fifth floor, but he couldn't make it up there yet. He collapsed onto a couch in the ground-floor reception area and waited for the nausea and fatigue to recede. He felt a little better than he had back there on the sidewalk, but he wasn't up to returning to work quite yet.

The reception area began to fade to white.

"Mr. Toyama."

He heard someone, somewhere, call his name. His vision grew hazy, like he was seeing everything through a film. He rubbed his eyes.

"Mr. Toyama."

The voice approached until it was right next to him. A hand patted him twice on the shoulder.

"Mr. Toyama, what's wrong? I've been calling your name."

He looked up toward the voice, alternately squinting and opening his eyes wide.

Fujisaki, a production assistant, and Yasui, a mixer, were standing beside him. Both of them worked for him.

Toyama gazed up at them as though at something

136

painfully bright. Fujisaki frowned. "I'm worried."

*What's wrong?*

He wanted to ask what was worrying Fujisaki, but he couldn't speak all of a sudden.

"Are you alright, Mr. Toyama?"

"S-s-sorry. C-could you bring me some—water?"

"Right away."

Fujisaki went to the vending machine in the corner and bought a sports drink, which he handed to Toyama. Toyama drank it down. Only then did he begin to feel a little more human. He said what he had tried to say before.

"What's wrong?"

"You'll have to come hear for yourself. I can't believe it."

Toyama stood up shakily and followed Fujisaki and Yasui to the elevator to the third floor, Studio 2. This was usually used for making classical recordings: it was perfect for strings, for chamber music and the like.

Fujisaki and Yasui had just yesterday gotten back from a recording session in another town. They'd rented a hall in the mountains that was popular for recording and taken the musicians up there: the clean, dry air made for a great sound.

They'd already reported to Toyama that the session had gone well. All that was left in terms of studio work was some editing. Then the album would be done, ready for release as a CD. It would hit the record stores soon.

"Is there a problem?"

Fujisaki held out a pair of headphones and said, "Just take a listen."

Toyama put on the headphones and sat down at the mixing table. At a look from him, Fujisaki hit play and the tape reel started moving.

He heard a pretty piano melody. Nothing wrong here. He flashed Fujisaki a puzzled look.

"Right there." Fujisaki rewound the tape and played it again. The piano was descrescendoing from mezzo forte to mezzo piano, but there was something else there, besides the piano. It was faint, but Toyama's trained ears were able to pick it out. His eyes started darting about the room. He was visibly shaken. He started to tremble.

"What do you think it is? It sounds like a baby crying to me."

A baby crying, weakly. But that wasn't all there was. Fujisaki might not have heard it, but Toyama did: somewhere behind the cries, there were words, floating in and out of hearing. There it was. He felt a rush of nostalgia as he recognized the voice.

*Toyama, I love you.*

He doubted Fujisaki or Yasui could hear it. All they'd be able to hear was the baby. And their thinking was probably that there must have been a baby in a car behind the hall or something, and that their mikes had picked up its crying.

*But that's not it. That's not what happened.* Toyama screamed the words, but only in his own mind.

"This is a problem, wouldn't you say, Mr. Toyama? What do you want to do? This is the master tape, and what's more it's the only take we've got. I could swear this sound wasn't there when we were recording."

Toyama rushed out of the studio, leaving Fujisaki shaking his head.

"Mr. Toyama—where are you going?"

At the door he turned around and gasped, "It's stuffy in here. I need to go get some air." It was all he could do just to get that much out.

He left the studio and went down the hall. While he waited for the elevator to arrive, he pressed his face against the window at the end of the hall and stared down at the street below. Shadow and light swirled in the bright afternoon sun. The street began to turn misty white—as if his retinas were clouding over, although he knew they weren't—and finally everything began to turn black. The cold sweat made his forehead slippery against the glass, a nasty feeling; it was an oily sweat.

Blacks and whites reversed, and all color drained from the world, except for a single point that hit Toyama's eye like an arrow. A woman, in a wrong-for-the-season lime-green dress.

He was reminded of that time in the sound booth in the playhouse, long ago, when despite being lost in his lovemaking with Sadako, the red light on the cassette deck in the corner caught his eye. Shining in the blackness like that, it only served to underscore the darkness.

This was like a strange transposition of that scene.

That lime-green dress was the only spot of natural color left in the graying landscape, and it made for a violent disharmony. It disrupted the monochrome world with a fearsome, storm-like force. That tiny green speck asserted rulership over all.

The elevator door opened. He went to the first floor and across the reception area. By the time he'd left the building, the world had regained its former color. But the pain that gripped Toyama's chest would not go away.

## 11

He was unbearably thirsty. He'd just drunk a whole can of sports drink, the one Fujisaki had given him, but the dryness in his throat was becoming unendurable.

He bought a lemon soda at a vending machine right outside the building and drank it. As he did he could feel how much his body needed the fluid, but he didn't even register it as a pleasant taste: it seemed to be converted directly to cold sweat. He threw away the half-drunk soda and began to walk.

Waiting for the elevator, looking out the window, he'd felt a dizziness, and a sense that the world was losing its color, and in the midst of it a single spot of bright green had caught his eye. Now as he walked aimlessly, his mind was still on that green glow.

The scene in the sound booth twenty-four years ago came back to him like yesterday. Partly it was because of the voice he'd just heard in the studio, that whisper lurking behind the baby's cries. The voice was Sadako's. It had to be.

Sounds and smells, he reflected, could be like sparks igniting an explosion of old memories. In this case, the previous twenty-four years had somehow been removed from his memory circuits—somehow the present moment was being fused with the time he spent with Sadako in the sound booth.

*That smell.*

He'd begun to worry about that odd smell in the sound booth. At first he hadn't even noticed it. But every time he entered the room it impinged on his consciousness a little more, until he'd decided he had to try and nail down its source.

He couldn't figure out how to describe the smell: it wasn't rotten or anything, but then again it wasn't exactly fragrant. It was pungent—not strong, exactly, but subtly stimulating to the olfactory membrane.

*Lemon.*

His mind hit on it at last. Maybe there was a lemon somewhere in the room. But if there was, it had to have been there for a while, in which case it would be rotten, and that wasn't the smell. It was something fresh, like something just peeled. Something not yellow, but still green with youth—something not yet ripe.

He searched the room. He opened every cabinet, searched every shelf, but found nothing. The only thing he discovered was that the dried-up umbilical cord that had been placed before the little altar as an offering was gone. He couldn't think of who might have taken it or when. As far as he knew, Sadako was the only other person aware of its existence, but it was hardly worth accusing her of taking it—in fact, he was kind of relieved the grotesque thing was gone. He was reluctant to bring it up with her at all.

So the umbilical cord was gone, and in its place was the faint scent of unripe lemon.

*The umbilical cord?*

Once, in a book, he'd seen a color photo of a twelve-week old fetus in the womb. It was curled up, arms and legs stuck out in front of it; its head was much bigger than its body. It was only five or six centimeters long, but it was recognizably human—it was even possible to tell what sex it was. You could see a tiny protrusion in the genital area.

What stuck in Toyama's memory was the thread connecting the little fetus to its mother. The umbilical cord was thicker than the fetus's limbs and lined with red veins; it twisted and looped around, fixed firmly to the placenta. It was this very important conduit that brought oxygen and nutrients to the fetus.

To the fetus, the womb was the entire world; the umbilical cord, then, was the sole connection between the fetus's world and the outside. In that sense it was an interface. Only when it left its mother's body would the fetus realize that there was another world outside the one it had been living in. Looking at the photo, Toyama had tried to imagine what a surprise that would be for the fetus. And it had struck him that, as long as you were inside, you could never know about the outside.

Walking along the sidewalk he was suddenly overcome by a feeling of strangulation centered on a spot just above his navel—his stomach, probably. Chill sweat continued to stream from his pores. The joints in his arms ached, and when he tried to raise them they wouldn't move. He could barely keep walking.

His heart beat violently.

A single fact flashed across his mind. *Everybody who heard Sadako's voice over the intercom from the sound booth twenty-four years ago died of heart disease... But I wasn't there. I didn't hear the tape.* He was desperate in his denial, but then another voice seemed to speak.

*But you heard it directly from her, didn't you? And the words came to you not through your tympanic membranes, but directly into your brain.*

That had to have been his imagination. He wasn't telepathic, and anyway, there was no such thing as words forcing their way directly into a person's mind.

*Toyama, I love you.*

They came back to him now, those precious words from his beloved. But now they brought with them terror, as well.

The seed of anxiety had been sown. Why were those same words present on the reel-to-reel tape in the studio? Why had Sadako whispered to him so insistently from behind the baby's crying? He had actually heard those words through the medium of tape: he felt terror, shock, anxiety, and nostalgia—it made no sense, but his love for Sadako flamed up again. Only the thinnest of lines separated terror and love for him now; his feelings of twenty-four years ago were back, the same as they ever were, but at the same time he could distinctly feel something wrong with his heart.

He could tell without even having to turn around: the girl in the green dress was on the sidewalk across the street, behind him. Her pace was somewhat quicker than his. He kept walking. He didn't know where he was going, or why he had to keep walking. He just pressed on, without looking back.

When the girl in the green dress was even with him, she crossed to his side of the street, threading her way between moving cars. He detected the fragrance of unripe lemon, the same as he'd smelled twenty-four years ago.

Now she was right next to him. She was close enough to reach out and touch. He stumbled, and the back of his hand brushed her arm. She was alive, sure enough. The touch of his hand confirmed it.

He glanced at the girl out of the corner of his eye. She was wearing a green one-piece dress with no sleeves—the season being what it was, he got chills just looking at her. It made her stand out among the passersby on the sidewalk. The way she asserted herself in a crowd hadn't changed at all.

Her whole body seemed to be saying, *Look! I'm here.*

Her hair fell to the middle of her back; her hands were so white as to be almost translucent. The nail on the first finger of one of her hands was split. He looked at her feet. She wore no stockings, just pumps on her bare feet; she had purple bruises on her ankles. She was tall, with a nicely balanced figure—that too was un-changed.

The cramping in his stomach got worse and worse, and Toyama couldn't keep his feet moving. He collapsed on the sidewalk against the girl in the green dress. It seemed that the world was starting to close in on him. His back came into contact with the girl's bare legs, his greasy sweat dampening her soft skin.

He stayed there like that for a while, cradled on her knees. Passersby looked down at him and said things, but he couldn't make out what.

He thought he heard the word *ambulance*, faintly. He didn't like all these people staring at him. He wanted to chase them away, but his body was like a steel bar. He couldn't move. All he wanted was to be still, cradled there on the girl's knees.

He tried to lift a hand and touch her cheek. No such luck. The desire raced in his mind like an engine in neu-tral. His mind and his body were separate now, and it frustrated him.

Sadako's face was before him now. He'd missed her so much. Now he was staring up at her face, still young, untouched by the intervening quarter century, and he didn't find it strange at all. She was supposed to be dead...but that didn't matter now. Why hadn't she aged? That didn't matter either. He was just happy to be able to touch her, alive like long ago. His happiness pushed aside his fear of impending death; he found he could endure the rapid collapse of the world upon him. He only wished he could be free of this pain squeezing his stomach.

Somewhere in the distance he could hear the approach of an ambulance. The air brought him the reverberations of its siren. His arms were immobile from his shoulders to his elbows, but he thought he could still move his fingers. His hand crawled toward Sadako, and managed to catch hold of her.

With her free hand, Sadako reached into her handbag and pulled out a small object wrapped in tissue paper; the tissue had turned brown in spots. She opened the tissue, took out what it enclosed, and laid it on Toyama's palm. He felt this had happened to him once before, somewhere: she'd plucked something up and laid it on his palm...

In order to see it, he tucked in his chin and looked down toward his waist. The object lay naturally on his palm, weighing virtually nothing.

He tried to pull his hand closer to get a better look at it. The trembling of his palm made the object vibrate as though it had a life of its own. He finally understood: it was an umbilical cord.

This one wasn't dried and shriveled like the one he'd seen twenty-four years ago: this had fresh blood on it. It had probably been cut no more than a week ago. It was the conduit between a womb and a mother's body, an interface between the inner world and the outer.

The umbilical cord looked strangely like it had been torn—the ends had clearly not been snipped by sharp scissors.

His field of vision had shrunk even further: now all he could see was Sadako's face. He had no way of knowing what was causing the symptoms now fast progressing through his body, but he had a vague premonition of death. It looked, ironically enough, like he was to be granted his wish of dying in Sadako's arms.

He tried to smile. He wanted Sadako to respond in kind, but she remained without expression.

Out of habit, Toyama's forefinger began to move. When it used to be time for him to play the theme music at the end of a show, he'd always focus himself by rubbing his thumb and forefinger together before pressing play.

Sadako opened her mouth and began to speak.

*What? What are you trying to say?*

But whatever she was about to say stopped at her throat, and never reached Toyama's consciousness. In the end, maybe the Girl in Black hadn't been trying to say anything at all.

*Play button, on.*

He moved his forefinger, then gently squeezed the umbilical cord. There was no longer any doubt in his mind whose it was.

*Sadako's been reborn.*

A moment later the lights went out, signaling that the curtain was about to fall for Toyama.

He heard applause, somewhere. And the many gazes that had been turned on him all simultaneously...

HAPPY BIRTHDAY

# 1

The images stopped. Reiko Sugiura sat there trying to bring her heartbeat under control, muttering to herself, *It's like watching a play or something.*

It was a perfectly understandable reaction.

Instead of donning the instrument-studded head-mounted display and data gloves to watch what she'd just watched, she'd simply gazed at a flat-panel monitor as the scenes unfolded within it. Reiko was pregnant, and any potentially disturbing stimulus was out of the question. Living someone else's life, dying someone else's death—the shock would be far too great. The experience of simulated death had been known to cause real psychological damage. That couldn't be good for the baby. Amano had recommended that Reiko use the monitor instead.

Prior to her viewing, Reiko had been given a lecture about the Loop project by Professor Toru Amano, a specialist in it. She'd thought she understood, but there was still a part of her that couldn't quite believe it. It was easy to get confused—she had to keep telling herself that the people on the monitor were not playing roles, but living out their lives. *They weren't acting...*

Still, now that it was over, it felt like she'd been

watching a TV show.

*Why is that*, she wondered. If she'd been shown a video of someone's everyday life, she probably wouldn't have found it stagy. That would depend, of course, but she'd probably feel like she was stealing a look at someone's life. Perhaps not—if it wasn't a mundane scene but instead some unusual incident that she saw, perhaps she'd feel like she was watching a movie or a play. Speaking of unusual, what she'd just seen certainly was that. First, a woman fell into an exhaust shaft on the roof of a building and there gave birth to a baby. The baby gnawed through its own umbilical cord, then climbed a rope up the side of the shaft, all by itself. There was no way it could have happened in real life. It was too strange. Then came the man's story. The baby grew into an adult woman in the space of a week, and the man died cradled on her knees. She'd once been his lover. Maybe it was precisely because Reiko understood his feelings so well and empathized with his story so much that she'd found it theatrical.

Amano turned off the monitor and waited for what she'd just seen to sink in. Then he asked, gently, "What do you think?"

Reiko repeated the words she'd muttered to herself.

"It's like I was watching a play or something."

Amano smiled and nodded. "The first time I viewed something in the Loop I had the same reaction."

His tone was generous. Judging by the stage he was at in his research career, he had to be in his late forties, but he looked much younger. His pale, plump face, with its silver-rimmed glasses, showed no trace of ill will. Reiko found herself relaxing in his presence.

He had a way of calming people down. She'd felt it in his voice when he'd telephoned her three days ago. Not much else could have brought her there, no matter how many times they'd asked.

When Amano, whom she'd never met, had called her, Reiko's depression had been at its worst. She'd lost, she could say without exaggeration, her reason for living. The embryo growing within her only symbolized her mounting anxiety. Her attachment to life was weakening.

She had a choice to make—to have the baby or not—but had no strength of will left to choose one option or the other. She simply passed the days carried forward by inertia. Suicide was an evident solution, but even it had retreated into the distance. Instead she lived on, watching indifferently, as through the eyes of another. Eventually she'd be ravaged by the Metastatic Human Cancer Virus; certain death awaited her and she lacked any means to resist it.

The only thing that gave her any hope was Kaoru Futami, the father of the child she was carrying. At least, he should have given her hope. Two months ago, he'd left on a journey into the American desert, determined to find a way to eradicate the cancer virus that had brought the human race to the edge of extinction. A month later, over the phone, he suggested that he'd found, or was about to find, something, and then disappeared. He was presumably still wandering through the wilderness on his motorcycle. She had no way of contacting him. A month of that was too long.

When he'd left, they'd made a promise. She could still remember how his voice had sounded as he'd said the words: *Let's meet again two months from now. Until then, you have to keep living, no matter what.*

The two months had passed. The fetus, three months along at the time of the promise, was now at five months. She'd had no word from Kaoru. How was she supposed to muster the hope to go on living, to have the child?

Reiko would turn thirty-four within the year. Perhaps this was her last chance to have a baby. She'd had her firstborn, a boy, at twenty-two, and she'd lost him in the worst possible way—suicide. This new life had been vouchsafed her around the very same time. Considering the timing, it was easy to imagine her first child being reborn as this one—all the more reason to take good care of it. But Reiko carried the MHC virus, and the child was sure to be born infected. What was the point of forcing it to live a life of suffering? Its father Kaoru had taken it upon himself to find a reason.

Then three days ago she'd gotten a call from a Mr. Amano at the Life Science Research Center who had something he wanted to talk to her about regarding Kaoru. She'd been doubtful. Amano had asked her to come to his lab, but she couldn't rouse herself to do it. It was probably her instinct for self-preservation kicking in; she couldn't handle any more bad news. Though Amano's voice was soft, it could be the sympathy and hesitation the bringer of bad news must always feel. Reiko's guard was up. The man might have something awful to tell her about Kaoru.

Amano would neither confirm nor deny her suspicions. He told her that it was something he couldn't hope to explain over the phone and implored her to come to the center. Finally, she'd allowed herself to be persuaded, and here she was.

In the reception area that Reiko was shown into, she received a brief explanation of a massive project known as the Loop. When she heard that Kaoru had sat in the same room to hear the same lecture from Amano, she began to feel a kind of intimacy with her surroundings.

The Loop, she learned, was a global project to create an entire world with the aid of over a million massively parallel supercomputers. A world, it was called, but it didn't exist anywhere in space, just as images projected onto a screen didn't possess any extension of their own. It was cyberspace. The scientists discovered that life did not occur within it naturally, but when they transplanted RNA into it—RNA, the basis of life in the real world—life forms began to evolve of their own accord. Perhaps because the source was the same, the biosphere came to be nearly identical to the real one.

Amano broke the Loop project down into bite-size chunks of information as he explained it to her. This wasn't a presentation to an academic gathering; all Reiko needed to get was the gist of it. Amano geared the explanation to her level of understanding, avoiding technical language as much as possible, and finally decided that she'd pick it up quicker if he showed it to her rather than just told her about it. He called up two scenes integral to the cancerization of the Loop world and had Reiko watch them. One concerned a young woman known as Mai Takano, pregnant though a virgin; she fell into an exhaust shaft on the roof of a building and there, in that constricted rectangular space, gave birth. The baby seemed to be in full possession of a will of its own from the very beginning. Tearing its umbilical cord with its gums, it crawled up into the outside world using a lifeline it had arranged for beforehand.

Reiko, pregnant herself, found the scene quite disturbing.

The next scene took her twenty-four years into the cyberworld's past and to an entirely different setting. But it had one character in common with the other scene: the baby that had crawled out of Mai Takano's womb. Sadako Yamamura.

The second sequence seemed like a coming-of-age story set among a troupe of actors. It had more of a plot than the first but still had its unrealistic elements. A woman's voice was recorded onto a reel of audiotape without the intervention of a recording device; everyone who heard the tape developed heart problems and died. That was the premise. Having heard a woman's voice and a baby's cry on a tape, the main character was confronted with death. But he was able to greet it just as he'd always hoped to, in the lap of Sadako Yamamura, the woman he'd been in love with twenty-four years earlier. A soap opera.

Having shown Reiko these two fragments and asked for her reaction, Amano added a bit of explanation.

"They look like television programs, but they're not. Those people really lived and died."

Reiko tried to think this through with an analogy of her own. Since the end of the last century there had been virtual reality games, some of them rather skillfully done; as a child she'd played a few of them. With the years the characters got smoother and more consistent in their details, evolving into something quite like people. They were characters in games, made by humans, so it wasn't accurate to say they were alive. The life forms in the Loop, though, had evolved on their own. They were life.

She spoke her thoughts. "So I should think of them as characters in a game come to life?"

Amano nodded.

"You can think of it like that if you want. The life forms in the Loop all have DNA. They're alive. As you've seen for yourself, they look just like humans. They're separated into male and female, they fall in love, they reproduce sexually."

Based on what she'd seen on the monitor, Amano seemed to be telling the truth. The second video had shown a man and a woman falling in love and engaging in a sexual act. There was jealousy, also—in that, too, they were just like humans.

The Loop functioned on the same principles and laws as the Earth, Reiko was told, and there was no room for doubt that she could find. The Loop consisted of patterns based on the properties of carbon, nitrogen, helium, and the rest of the 111 elements that made up the universe, Amano said. Although Reiko couldn't imagine what that actually meant in terms of a computer system, she felt she more or less understood in her own way.

The scientific questions didn't interest Reiko. Loop beings lived in the Loop system, and that was enough for her. What interested her was Kaoru, the father of her child. Amano knew Kaoru. Why was he going on and on about this Loop thing?

Reiko remembered something Kaoru had once said to her.

*Reality might just be a kind of virtual space, you know.*

No, that wasn't precisely it—he'd actually said, in no uncertain terms, that reality *was* virtual.

Prior to the birth of the universe time and space did not exist. It was impossible to imagine such a situation—no time or space. Presented with the relationship between Loop and the real world, however, the idea became easier to envision. Thinking of the universe as a virtual reality removed the contradiction. Of course, that didn't mean that reality was just a computer simulation—it was something completely different, far beyond humanity's comprehension, operated by an unknown power. But with that caveat, there was no reason not to think of reality as a virtual space, no valid argument against it.

She recalled Kaoru saying something along those lines.

She tried to change the subject. "But..."

"I know." Amano raised his hands as if to stop her, and his expression said that he wanted her to indulge him just a little while longer. He did seem to make a greater effort to get to the core of the problem and spoke of the Metastatic Human Cancer Virus.

"The Loop world is not unrelated to the MHC virus that's destroying our world."

Reiko's body stiffened and she let out a little cry.

It was the MHC virus that had visited such unhappiness on her family. The virus had the demonic ability to turn cells cancerous and to cause them to metastasize and permeate the whole body. There was no end to the hatred she bore this enemy. Cancer had devoured her husband two years ago; two months ago, her son Ryoji had thrown himself from the window of the hospital where he was undergoing chemotherapy and hating it. Reiko had fallen in love with Kaoru, her son's tutor, and together they'd conceived the child now in her womb. Reiko herself was a carrier of the virus, and inevitably that meant Kaoru had become infected as well. Moreover, Kaoru's father was in the final stages of his own cancer, undergoing treatment at the same hospital;

Kaoru's mother was another carrier. On every direction Reiko was surrounded by misery, the MHC virus the cause of it all. Worldwide, the infected—concentrated in Japan and America—numbered in the millions. It was spread through blood and lymph, but scientists were discovering other routes as well. The disease was starting to affect animals and plants, and people were starting to whisper that this was going to be the end of all life on Earth.

"It's become clear to us that the Metastatic Human Cancer Virus originated in the Loop. It was Kaoru who figured it out."

It was the first time Amano had spoken Kaoru's name since she'd arrived. Reiko's body reacted to that first—she could feel veins twitch deep within her body.

*Then he did it after all.*

She rejoiced in his accomplishment, although she had no idea whether isolating the source of the virus helped treat it. She was simply glad for him.

"Does that mean you've found a cure?"

Amano didn't answer her question. Instead, he launched into another long explanation.

"The two scenes you just witnessed represent, if you will, the beginnings. As you saw, the individual known as Sadako Yamamura has the ability to record her voice onto an audiotape solely by willing it. It shouldn't be possible, according to the scientific laws of the Loop world. At the risk of repeating myself, our world and the virtual space of the Loop world are ruled by exactly the same physical principles. You also saw that this Sadako Yamamura dies once, only to effect her own rebirth twenty-four years later through Mai Takano's womb. This too is a phenomenon that common sense tells us is impossible. Some say it's the result of a computer virus, but the truth is we don't know the actual cause yet, and knowing it might not help us solve the problem anyway. And the problem is: how do we deal with the virus that was thus produced, regardless of how it came to be?"

Reiko was confused. By that logic, isolating the origin of the MHC virus didn't mean they had learned how to vanquish it. It meant Kaoru's discovery had been in vain; she didn't want to think it.

Reiko confronted Amano with her doubts. He gave her an earnest answer.

"It's like asking why we exist. We do exist, you and I, here and now as human beings. Why do humans exist at all? That question and its answer are of a different order from the question of how to manage society and improve it. Why do humans take the form they do, why are they ruled by desires? Knowing the answers won't necessarily help us learn how to live better. We simply have to accept what's here and manage things as they are.

"Please don't misunderstand me, though. Kaoru's discovery was truly significant. It allowed us to describe the virus's evolutionary process.

"Are you with me? Let's go back to the beginning. There were warning signs. Sadako Yamamura, being the unique character she is, produces a videotape that kills anybody who watches it in a week's time. The only way to evade death is to make a copy of the videotape and to show it to someone who hasn't yet seen it. Pursued to its conclusion, this means the videotape's numbers should increase exponentially. Along the line, as a result of some mischief, the tape mutates, evolves, metamorphoses into other media. It spreads like wildfire—or like a virus infecting its victims. In fact, a kind of virus appears in the bodies of those who watch the videotape. In the Loop world they call it the ring virus. Women who contract the virus while ovulating become pregnant without insemination and give birth to Sadako Yamamura.

"You see now. The first scene you witnessed was just that: Mai Takano, infected with the ring virus, giving birth to Sadako."

Reiko felt relief. She couldn't help but think that whatever calamity might have befallen the Loop, it had nothing to do with her. As she listened, only half believing, to Amano's story, she tried to imagine a videotape that killed you a week after you watched it, such a videotape spreading through the world, creating a virus, attacking a woman's womb and implanting a new life form. If that ever happened in reality, people would panic—no telling what they'd do. Rumors feeding on rumors, things would deteriorate at an accelerating rate.

"So what happened?" She was ready for this to end.

"The Loop world lost its diversity. Everything was

assimilated to the Sadako Yamamura genotype, became cancerous, and died. Without biodiversity, extinction is only a matter of time. Just as the Loop was dying out, however, the project was frozen for budgetary reasons. That was twenty years ago."

The words "cancerous" and "extinction" piqued Reiko's curiosity. The conversation finally seemed to be arriving at reality.

She hugged herself, rubbing her upper arms with her palms. "Sounds just like the real world. Kind of frightening."

"Exactly. Reality and the virtual space reflect each other. They correspond to each other."

"Do you mean they're influencing each other?"

"You could put it that way."

"Like—like a mother and a fetus?"

"That's quite an apt comparison." Amano sounded impressed.

Reiko was just trying to apply the far-fetched tale to herself, to find some way to wrap her mind around it. It had occurred to her that Loop was somewhat similar to the womb. It was a world of its own, a space housing a life created by parents. A mother's state of health affected her fetus. The reverse was also possible. And it wasn't just a question of physical condition, either. A mother had an emotional and mental influence over her fetus that wasn't always reducible to explanations via matter. If the mother was happy and at peace, the fetus breathed peacefully; if the mother was frustrated or angry, the fetus's heart rate increased. An illness in one could cause grave damage in the other.

That was Reiko's thinking as she asked her next question. "Did Loop's extinction affect the real world? Is that what happened?"

"Yes. It exerted an invisible influence. But apart from that, there's another factor at work, which we've been able to study. It seems that the Loop world's virus invaded the real world, where it evolved into the MHC virus."

Tabling for the moment the mechanism by which a virus from the virtual world could function in the real one, Amano began to tell her why the ring virus had crossed over into the real world. What Reiko heard next floored her.

"Among those in the Loop world infected with the ring virus was an individual named Ryuji Takayama. He's the only being ever to cross from the virtual world into ours.

"This Takayama dies in the Loop world. But Professor Eliot—Chris Eliot, the father of the Loop project—decided to bring him back to life in the real world by refabricating his genetic information. It wasn't possible to take him apart on a molecular level and recreate him, so the only option was to embed his genetic information in a fertilized egg and to arrange for him to be born into this world as an infant. Unfortunately, he carried the ring virus. At present the thinking is that there must have been an accident during the DNA breakdown-reconstitution phase at which point it escaped from an intestinal bacterium. The hypothesis, and it's well-founded, is that the ring virus mutated into the MHC virus. A comparison of the DNA base sequences of the two viruses reveals a shocking degree of similarity."

Amano stopped talking and fixed Reiko with a gaze. Reiko noticed the change and braced herself.

"Ryuji Takayama was reborn into the real world twenty years ago."

Amano seemed to place special emphasis on *twenty years*, and Reiko wondered why. That was Kaoru's age, she noted.

"I think it would be quicker if you had a look at this." Amano called up a third scene on the monitor. "Please don't be shocked. That is—I'm sorry... No matter what I say, I know it'll be a shock, and in your condition... But I don't know what to say."

He seemed not to relish the responsibility that had become his. But Amano's expression cleared and he continued:

"Now, watch. This is Ryuji Takayama, of the Loop world."

He pressed some buttons on the keyboard and enlarged the scope.

It was a rear view of Takayama as he sat in an office at the university studying logic. The vantage point gradually rotated until they were seeing him from the front. Still seated at his desk, Takayama raised his head and looked up at the ceiling. Amano zoomed in on his face.

Reiko looked at the image on the screen and uttered a name, and it was not "Takayama." But her face expressed none of the shock Amano had expected. She simply reacted as anyone facing the image of a loved one onscreen might: she'd called his name out of habit. She did not, could not, comprehend, not at once, that Ryuji Takayama and Kaoru Futami were the same person.

## 2

It didn't matter where Kaoru's DNA came from.

Reiko didn't care. Life emerged from nothingness. The child inside her—before the sperm fertilized the egg, it hadn't existed.

The only things that mattered, Reiko felt, were acts. Like those passionate moments with Kaoru, stolen while her son Ryoji was off getting tested for chemotherapy, when they could use his room like a hotel—the impulse had been a pure one, a loving one. They hadn't acted on physical instinct alone unaccompanied by feeling. Their acts had been driven by love, and the result was that she carried new life within her womb.

*But still.*

It wasn't that she didn't understand the concept. Given that the Loop life forms had DNA, she was prepared to accept that science could reconstruct them. But still...it was like being told all of a sudden that Kaoru was a cyborg or something.

She'd had intercourse with Kaoru a number of times in that hospital room, with the curtains open and the brilliant afternoon sunlight shining in. There in the bright light they had examined each other's organs, lapped each other's fluids, felt each other's pulses against their mucous membranes. She'd taken his semen into her mouth. She could remember its bitter taste, the feel of it on her tongue. It tasted like something secreted from a living body; it tasted like life.

Reiko had only a general grasp of the mechanics of one of his sperm reaching her egg and fertilizing it. If she did understand every detail, it wouldn't have changed what surfaced in her memory now, which was the act, and a recollection of the emotions of which it had been the manifestation. The new life had been created out of thoughts, out of will.

*I love you.*

That didn't change upon learning Kaoru's provenance.

Amano, meanwhile, had no way of knowing that Reiko was occupied with confirming her love for Kaoru. As a scientist, all that was on his mind was whether she understood the process.

"I get it," she said. "Kaoru's birth did not result from the sexual union of his parents."

Her response reassured Amano somewhat. If she got that much, he would be spared the barrage of questions. They'd just saved a lot of time. "I'm glad you do," he said.

What Reiko wanted to know was not the "why" of the beginnings of his existence, but the current progress of it. In short, where was he and what was he doing?

"Where is Kaoru now?" she asked Amano.

He gave a little sigh and shook his head. He looked

at his wristwatch, assumed a thoughtful pose, then slowly stood up and ordered two cups of coffee over an intercom. Reiko thought his actions affected. She had a bad feeling about what was coming next.

At length a young woman appeared with the coffee. Amano distractedly brought his to his lips and said, without meeting Reiko's eyes, "Please, have some coffee."

Then, haltingly, he began to tell her, not where Kaoru was, but about a scientific device called the Neutrino Scanning Capture System, NSCS or Neucap for short. It used phase shifts caused by neutrino vibrations to make a digital record of a living creature in three dimensions, down to the last detail, including the state of its proteins and electrical fields. Through neutrino irradiation, the machine also made a record of brain activity—thoughts, emotions, memories—capturing literally every piece of information and storing it as data.

Reiko was only half listening, but when Amano mentioned that the NSCS was located in North America, deep underground at the Four Corners, where the states of New Mexico, Arizona, Utah, and Colorado meet, she looked up with a start. That was where Kaoru had been headed on his quest to find out about the MHC virus.

"That's where Kaoru is, isn't it?" She clung to the idea.

Amano merely looked uncomfortable. He dithered, unwilling to confirm or deny her guess. Reiko watched him wordlessly, commanding herself to be calm no matter what he said next.

"It was discovered that the telomerase sequence in Kaoru's DNA was not TTAGGG. What this means is that while the MHC virus produced the TTAGGG telomerase sequence and attached it to the end of his DNA like it does to all its victims, in Kaoru's case it was unstable, breaking down almost immediately. In short, he had perfect resistance to the MHC virus."

"You mean, Kaoru won't come down with MHC?"

"That's correct. The virus doesn't cancerize his cells."

"That's wonderful..."

But the pounding in Reiko's chest would not subside. Instead, that "Neucap" had taken root in her imagination, where it was now glowing, pale and ghostly.

"I'm not sure how else to put it. It was what the whole world had been waiting for. The key to defeating the MHC virus was found in Kaoru's own body."

Reiko thought back over things Kaoru had said and done. He must have sensed, intuitively, that he was going to make a huge contribution to discovering the origin of the MHC virus, and a cure to it. He'd carried that destiny around with him since birth—he'd been on a kind of mission.

"So he's going to be able to help find a treatment."

"Absolutely. That's putting it mildly. His complete biodata has been analyzed, and we're quite close to perfecting a breakthrough treatment. It's all thanks to Kaoru."

*Complete biodata.*

The words caught her ear. From the course of the conversation, it wasn't hard to imagine that Kaoru had submitted himself to the NSCS. But the direction Amano was taking the discussion worried her. He hadn't volunteered any information as to what had happened to Kaoru's body in the process of providing his complete biodata. The professor was being evasive on that point.

"Did you use this NSCS on Kaoru?"

"Yes." Amano nodded.

"What happens to someone's body when the NSCS is used on it?"

"Kaoru's body was completely sterilized and he was placed in a tank of purified water, where he floated in the center of a dome two hundred meters in diameter. Neutrinos were shot at him from every point along the sphere's surface. They passed through his body and reached the opposite point on the sphere, in the process accumulating information about his molecular structure."

She didn't care about the mechanism. Her voice rose in frustration.

"What happened to his body?"

"In order to get his complete biodata, it was necessary to expose him to radiation intense enough to break down his cells, and as a result..."

Reiko's hair flew about as she leaned abruptly forward.

"That is, what happened was..."

Reiko nearly screamed.

Amano seemed to be trying to impress upon her that he bore no responsibility in the matter—his voice grew angry, although his anger had no particular object.

"Listen to me. As a result, his body was liquefied. It was destroyed."

"Liquefied? Destroyed?" In a daze she repeated the words. She tried and failed to imagine that happening to a body. What happened to his life? She knew the answer to that, but she couldn't accept it.

She started to speak, but bit back the words. Her mouth opened and closed helplessly; she looked like she was about to hyperventilate. Amano took pity on her and pronounced.

"Kaoru is dead to this world."

Reiko and Amano stared at each other for a long time. Amano couldn't avert his gaze from her big eyes, turned slightly down at the corners. He'd have to take her emotional explosion head-on.

Reiko was the first to look away. Tears welled up in her eyes; the next moment she'd collapsed face down on the table, heedless as some of her hair landed in the coffee.

Her voice was muffled as she moaned, "I can't believe it..."

She didn't know what to say. Two years ago she'd lost her husband to MHC; two months ago her son, afflicted with the same disease, had killed himself. And now—or rather, a month ago—her lover, the father of the child she was carrying, had also departed this world, and in a manner she couldn't even begin to describe. What a catastrophe—she could feel her will to live withering away.

*I can't take it anymore.*

She'd already been sick of life before coming to the research center. Now that Amano had informed her of Kaoru's death, she could feel her helplessness metamorphosing into a distinct death wish. She had to staunch this sadness at its root, and the only way to do that was to destroy the body from which her emotions sprang.

It didn't matter that Kaoru's biodata could cure her own condition. She could take no more. She might overcome her cancer and live several decades more, but her sorrow would stay with her forever. She didn't want to live in such a state. This she could say with perfect certainty.

*No more.*

She stood up. As she did, she knocked over her cup and spilled coffee on her lap, but she didn't seem to care as she whirled around and headed for the door.

"Where are you going?"

Amano pursued her, grabbing her by the wrist.

"That's enough."

"No, it's not. I have more to tell you."

"I know all I need to know."

"You don't know anything yet."

Reiko reached for the doorknob, ignoring him. But Amano held her arm. In pain, she yelled, "Leave me alone!" Anger was unusual for her.

Amano couldn't back down. Kaoru had had his mission; Amano now had his. He had promises to keep—to Dr. Eliot, but more importantly to Kaoru.

"Won't you please calm down and listen? I promised Kaoru I'd do this."

Reiko held still. She stopped resisting and waited for Amano's next words. The line about promising Kaoru seemed to have worked.

"A promise..."

"Yes. It's my task to bring you and Kaoru face to face. Before he left on his journey, Kaoru made me and Dr. Eliot promise. I have a duty to follow his instructions. It's my way of repaying him for what he's done— save humanity, no less. What I'm going to do is call up the appropriate moment and bring you and Kaoru face to face."

"Face to face? You mean...I can meet him?"

"Yes, yes, of course. He's alive and well on the other side."

Reiko half turned around, coffee dripping from her hair. She looked pale, haggard.

"Please, sit down." Amano indicated the sofa.

It took a little while for Reiko to suppress her emotions and return to normal. She paused for a moment, slowly fixing her hair and face, then followed Amano's suggestion and sank onto the sofa.

Amano kept looking at his watch. It bothered Reiko.

"Are we alright for time?" she asked.

"What? Oh, it's just that we've got an appointment in ten minutes."

"Who's your appointment with?"

"Kaoru."

Reiko started to feel confused again. What validity was there to an appointment with someone who'd been dead for a month?

Amano tried, gently, to clear up any misunderstandings.

"First of all, I'd like you to know that Kaoru freely chose to undergo NSCS."

"Did he know it would kill him?"

"He did. The NSCS digitizes the emotions of the subject at the precise moment of scanning. It wouldn't work if we tied someone up and forced them to undergo neutrino irradiation. When someone is full of fear and hatred, or denial, the body stiffens and we can't get a reading of their natural biodata. So I must ask you to fully accept the fact that Kaoru went in of his own free will. He welcomed death with a serene heart and an un-ruffled state of mind so that we could get an accurate scan of his biodata. He had the most exalted of motivations. He was sacrificing himself to save the human race. And let me be more specific. Kaoru particularly wanted to save you, and the child you carry, and his parents."

Amano's words weighed on her. If Kaoru had died for her and her child, suddenly her life became a much more important thing. She felt more valuable in her own eyes.

Amano continued:

"Kaoru's death meant two things. First, as I keep re-iterating, it enabled us to utilize his biodata to find a cure for MHC. Second, digitizing his molecular information allowed us to bring him back to life within the Loop world.

"The cancerization of the Loop world and the cancerization of the real world relate to each other in subtle, intimate ways that you expressed through the metaphor of the mother and the fetus. Restoring biodiversity is the only real solution to the problems of both biospheres. Kaoru died in this world and left us his biodata, and we'll make the fullest use of it. We needed him to come back to life in the Loop and to bear the burden of returning that world, too, to its normal state of biodiversity. In short, he needed to carry out the duties of a god. His death was simultaneously a departure into the Loop world. When he arrived, the Loop project—which had been frozen for twenty years—was reactivated. It got a new start, from a point just this side of extinction."

"Can't you bring him back to life in this world, then?"

"We can't restore him just as he was. It's possible to create a new life with Kaoru's DNA using cloning technology, which developed at the end of the last century. I'm sure I don't have to explain to you that while such a being would have Kaoru's DNA, he would have different life experiences—he'd be a different person. However, the Kaoru that was brought back to life within the Loop is exactly the same as the Kaoru who lived here—the same thought patterns, the same emotions, and the same memories."

"So you're saying he remembers me."

"Of course he does."

It finally sank in that Kaoru was alive in the other world. But that still didn't change the fact that he'd died. As long as he was in the virtual world, they couldn't interact physically. They couldn't communicate—or at least, she couldn't see how. All she'd be able to do was watch him on a screen, as though he were some character in a television show. Wasn't it worse to have her loved one so close at hand and be unable to touch him?

"Can the Loop beings see us?"

It was the next logical question. She knew, because she had experienced it twice now, that she could observe the Loop world. But even as a layperson she could surmise that the reverse might not be so easily accomplished.

"No, they can't. Just like we can't peek into the world of the gods."

But the image that came into Reiko's mind was not of god and man.

A few days ago Reiko had gone to see her obstetrician, and the doctor had shown her the fetus. She'd lain down on a bed and hiked up her blouse to expose her belly, and the doctor had applied the ultrasound to her skin, summoning an image of the fetus on the monitor. The doctor had talked to her about the baby's development. Reiko had been struck by how easily the echo machine showed her the inside of her womb. Here, too, the comparison of the Loop to a womb proved helpful to her. A mother could see the fetus in her womb, but the fetus could not be conscious of its mother in her entirety. Perception in this case was a one-way street.

And so Reiko had no trouble accepting the fact that while the real world could look in on the Loop, the reverse was impossible.

"I understand. Now let me meet him."

She intentionally used an expression that implied they'd be in the same space even though she knew that she'd see him and not the reverse. She wanted to feel like they'd be together, even temporarily. If only she could recapture the feeling of his skin touching hers...

"Alright. It's about time we left this room. I think Kaoru has things he wants to tell you. He was evidently quite insistent that Dr. Eliot promise him this meeting. He didn't want to leave you a message by holographic memory. I think he just wanted to feel for an instant that you and he were in the same place at the same time, to feel that you were there before his eyes."

They went into a laboratory divided down the middle by a standing screen. Amano went to a computer and input a time and a place. Reiko sat where she was told. He asked if she wanted to use a helmet display and data gloves.

"What happens if I use them?"

"The experience will be three-dimensional. Altogether more realistic. The data gloves will allow you to touch Kaoru's body."

Without a moment's hesitation, she chose to use them.

She put on the equipment and waited for the time to come. Two minutes to go. She steadied her breathing and wiped the coffee from her hair with a handkerchief, arranging it behind her head. She knew he wouldn't be able to see her, but her feminine instincts insisted.

It had been two months since she'd last seen his face. Now he was dead—seeing him would feel like they'd put TV cameras in heaven or something. Her anticipation mounted. She wanted to see him calm and at peace. She thought it might reassure her, to a degree.

# 3

In Loop time, it was nearly two pm on June 27, 1991. The latitude and longitude coordinates were aligned precisely as they should be. Reiko was about to experience the Loop world in three dimensions, sight and sound.

As the system started, she could feel that she was being taken to another place. Her surroundings were blurry white, and countless droplets of moisture floated all around her. Her body was thrust between them. She seemed to be floating in clouds and her body felt light. She was not afraid. In fact, she felt quite comfortable, as if she'd obtained a new, freer body.

It didn't take her long to realize that those were actual clouds obscuring her field of vision. She made her way forward until she passed through a rent in the clouds to the other side. She found herself looking down at a coastline, a peninsula extending out into the sea. Her point of view descended until the intricate coastline became so clear she felt she could reach out and touch it. The land sloped steeply down to the ocean, leaving precious little space for the seaside pines and only a thin strip of beach.

A paved road wound its way through the hills, shining up at her grayly. The Loop world's sun seemed to be at her back; she couldn't see it, but she could see the reflection of its rays on the road, and on the waves, glittering. She was able to sense that the sun was there behind her.

She saw a human figure on an animal track that veered off the road toward the ocean. At first she couldn't tell what it was looking for as it wandered back and forth along the pine-covered hillside. Was it trying to find a clear field of vision? Or someplace where it could bask in the rays of the sun as they broke through the clouds?

Finally the figure sat down in a grassy clearing on the slope. It then looked straight up at where Reiko's "eyes" should be.

All was silent, except for the surf in the distance and the wind that surrounded her. As her vantage point lowered and the ground rose to meet her she got a curious sense of spatial relationships. It wasn't like landing in an airplane; it was slower than that. She'd never parachuted, but she imagined this was what it felt like.

The figure sitting there holding his knees was known in her world by the name Kaoru Futami, while in the Loop he was called Ryuji Takayama. Time in the Loop moved six times faster than in the real world; the month Reiko had spent since last talking with him corresponded to six months there. But that wasn't important. What mattered right now was that Kaoru, too, was aware that Reiko was right in front of him.

She looked down on him from a height of several meters, gazing at his forehead, his nose, the strong-willed set of his mouth. He smiled up as if searching for Reiko's face floating there in the sky. He knew, he had to know, that she was looking at him.

Reiko stayed where she was for a while and allowed memories of Kaoru to pass through her mind. They'd spent so little time together, shared so few spaces. The hospital was practically the only place where they'd voiced their love for each other, but Reiko's son had committed suicide there. Pleasant memories of the place coexisted with sorrowful ones.

Reiko searched for recollections that were purely of Kaoru, fleshing them out, comparing them with the face she was now seeing. Kaoru was right there in front of her, but she closed her eyes.

An image of herself and Kaoru replayed in her mind. He was walking along the hospital corridor. When he saw her, his face lit up with a joy he didn't even try to conceal. She missed that innocence of his. She could re-call the warmth of his skin as he hesitantly touched her—as he picked her up with ease and carried her to the bed. She recalled how they had stood looking over the city from the top floor of the hospital, talking about what they'd do if they could conquer the illness, losing themselves in unrealizable dreams.

*Do I want to capture those memories? Do I want to re-experience them?*

No, that wasn't it. She wanted to go forth with

Kaoru into the future. But he was dead. He didn't really exist anymore. He wasn't anyone she could go forth with.

But when she opened her eyes, he was even closer. He moved his lips. Clearly he was trying to say something, but she couldn't hear him—was the machine malfunctioning? She told Amano, who was sitting beside her, watching her, and sure enough, it seemed there had been a mistake. He adjusted the automatic translator so that Kaoru's words could reach her.

Kaoru was looking straight upward, and his gaze bristled with determination. He was saying something, in simple, clearly enunciated words. At first it sounded like static, but as Amano made the requisite adjustments Reiko began to make them out. As a result of passing through the translator, Kaoru's voice sounded subtly different, but she understood what he was saying.

"It's going—to be—alright."

He gave a big nod, as if to confirm it with himself.

*It's alright.*

What was alright? Was he beating a drum for the world he'd given his life to protect? Where did he get that kind of confidence? Yet, Reiko could tell that her attitude toward life, which had already undergone such drastic changes in the few hours since she'd come to the research center, was approaching a new conclusion.

Kaoru had sacrificed himself to save Reiko and the child she carried, and now he sat before them saying, "It's alright." With him affirming the world, she had no grounds for doubt.

*I'll live.*

The thought pierced her body. She'd begun to lose the sense that she was really alive, but now, in a way that transcended all causes, she suddenly had it back.

Just before Kaoru had set out for the desert, Reiko had been hinting at suicide, and he'd extracted a promise from her.

*Let's meet again two months from now. Until then, you have to keep living, no matter what.*

His promise was that in two months he'd reappear, a solution in hand. He'd kept his promise.

Reiko moved her hands, encased in data gloves, and touched Kaoru. She placed her hands on his shoulders and felt his prominent shoulder blades, covered in well-toned muscle. He was just the same.

Kaoru rearranged his legs so that he was sitting Indian-style and stretched out his hands. Reiko grasped them; he didn't respond. Of course he didn't. He couldn't see her. But she didn't give up.

She desperately repeated the motion, again and again, hoping that her desire to communicate might move him. She ran her hands up his arms, entwined her fingers in his. Meanwhile Kaoru waved, scratched his head, and in general did exactly the opposite of what she wanted. Finally, he seemed to realize something. He mused, arms hanging at his sides, then held out his hands again. It was a gesture of surrender; her will, not his, would determine the course of this.

Reiko placed her hands on his and left them there for a while so that they could begin to feel each other's intentions. She was afraid that any sudden movement might sever her connection to him. Then, carefully, she moved a hand. His hand made a corresponding movement. He'd sensed her. She was sure that Kaoru could intuit that he was holding her hands even if he couldn't see her.

Reiko cautiously placed his hands on her chest, then slowly moved them downward. Their clasped hands were like an umbilical cord linking the real world with the Loop. She guided his hands downward, to her belly, to her navel.

"Can you hear it?"

She hoped that the tiny heartbeat was felt against his skin.

Kaoru nodded, and said again, "It's going to be alright."

Perhaps his voice reached the fetus. It moved in her like never before.

# 4

When she walked through the hospital doors, Reiko's heart was a tangle of complicated emotions. This was the hospital where her son Ryoji had jumped to his death, so she'd expected it to affect her badly. She anticipated grief, but to her surprise the first memory that came to her was of meeting Kaoru.

She went up to the third floor and crossed the spacious lobby to the elevator for the B wing. The third floor was where the cafeteria was, overlooking the courtyard. Reiko had first met Kaoru there.

He'd been looking at her, but men were always looking at her. She'd shot him a pointed glance, but it didn't affect him in the least. In fact, his gaze grew more determined and it soon became impossible for her to ignore it. A few days later, she had the chance to speak with him. Once she learned what kind of person he was—once she glimpsed his ideals—she found herself attracted to him as a woman. It was partly to increase her contact with him that she asked him to tutor her son.

But then they became lovers, and as a direct result of that, her son resorted to killing himself. She couldn't blame him for despairing, knowing how painful the tests were for him, while she and Kaoru were just waiting for him to leave the room so they could indulge their passion for each other. He'd begun to feel like an intruder, and that had robbed him of his last hope.

"I'll be gone, so you two knock yourselves out."

His suicide note had bound her like some spell.

In the period immediately following his suicide, she had tried to tell herself that he would have died anyway of MHC. Now that Kaoru's biodata had revealed how to fight the disease, Ryoji's death affected her more than ever. If only he'd endured a little longer, the techniques made possible by Kaoru's sacrifice might have saved him.

The elevator stopped on the seventh floor, and Reiko stepped out into the hallway and looked around. For a moment, she lost her orientation. Space seemed to warp around her. Halfway down the hallway was an emergency door, behind which a stairway stretched up and down into the darkness. Reiko's neural cells resisted remembering anything more. On the landing there was a small triangular window that could be opened from the inside or the outside in an emergency. One evening three months ago, Ryoji had jumped from that window, turning himself into a red stain on the concrete below.

Her meeting with Kaoru, her parting with Ryoji—they'd both happened in the same place. No matter where she looked, for her, the hospital was a tangle of memories.

Though she hadn't regained her composure, Reiko looked at the scrap of paper in her hand, confirmed the number written on it, and knocked on a door.

"Come in."

The answer was immediate, as if she was expected just then, and from behind the door she heard the whisper of cloth rubbing against cloth.

She opened the door to find Hideyuki Futami leaning against the wall in an unnatural posture, his pajamas open in the front. The room smelled of bodily excretions. Reiko took a couple of steps into the room and shut the door behind her. She reminded herself that the smell belonged to Kaoru's father, and it ceased to bother her as much.

"Pleased to meet you. I'm Reiko Sugiura."

Hideyuki moved away from the wall and a smile lit up his face. "I'm glad you've come. Please," he said, indicating a metal folding chair.

Hideyuki had known she'd be visiting him—she'd contacted him ahead of time. He already knew that his son Kaoru and she had been lovers, and that she was pregnant. Kaoru had confessed it all to him just before he left.

Reiko knew that the joy lighting up Hideyuki's face was for her and the child she carried. Though this was their first meeting, she recognized the sincerity in his face.

She took a seat in the chair Hideyuki offered her. She examined his features, without precisely meaning to. She was curious to see if his face revealed how well he was holding up against the cancer. She also felt a certain gratitude toward him for raising Kaoru.

Kaoru had come into the world via an implantation

of chromosomes from the virtual world into a fertilized egg, which had then been placed in a woman's uterus. At the same time, he'd grown up as the son of Hideyuki Futami and his wife. He may not have inherited Hideyuki's DNA, but Hideyuki had raised Kaoru with care as his only child. Meanwhile, the life within Reiko had inherited Kaoru's DNA.

Given that its ultimate source was an artificial life form, Reiko might have been expected to feel strange about the child, as if she were carrying an alien thing within her. But she found she was able to accept the facts with no qualms whatsoever. She could feel the immense strength of will that had been passed down from Hideyuki to Kaoru and now to her child. Her rendezvous with Kaoru a month ago had confirmed that.

Kaoru's message had enabled Reiko to find the will to go on living. She felt that a face-to-face meeting with Hideyuki, who was making a miraculous recovery thanks to information Kaoru's sacrifice had made available, should strengthen her determination.

And that was why she couldn't stop gazing at Hideyuki now with curiosity and gratitude, and concern for his condition.

"You look like you're doing well."

Of course, her comment was not informed by the way he'd looked before, but Kaoru had told her all about his condition: how the cancer had moved decisively into his lungs and how, since further surgery was impossible, all that was left was to wait for death. It had been a tug of war between life and death, but judging by Hideyuki's appearance now, life seemed to be winning.

"I feel good. I feel so light these days. Well, I suppose that might just be because I've had so many organs removed." He laughed.

They proceeded to tell each other what had been happening in their lives lately. Reiko drew for the overjoyed Hideyuki a verbal picture of how Kaoru had been reborn in the Loop world and how he'd given her his bold message. Hideyuki, ever the scientist, used his body as an example to explain how they'd taken the telomerase sequence from Kaoru's DNA and introduced it into the cells of MHC patients with groundbreaking results. He was trying to comfort Reiko, who was a carrier of the disease herself, and it worked. The MHC virus was no longer something to fear.

Finally, Hideyuki's interest turned to Reiko's condition.

"Is everything going well?"

Reiko smiled and patted her belly. At the moment there were no problems; the fetus was growing well. Hideyuki asked when she was due, and she told him the truth. The date was about three months ahead, and rapidly approaching. But when he asked about the baby's sex, she gave the vaguest of answers.

"I wonder."

In truth, she knew the baby's sex. Last month, when she'd gone to the obstetrician for an ultrasound, she'd looked at the monitor and seen a cute little protuberance right where the baby's legs joined.

*Ah—a boy.*

Lying there on the bed watching the screen, she'd actually uttered the words. The doctor maintained a studious silence, but a nurse was standing nearby and her expression indicated that Reiko was right.

She had decided not to let Hideyuki know that it was a boy. She didn't want him to expect the child to be a reincarnation of Kaoru. She decided that ambiguity was what was called for.

Reiko gathered herself to leave, and Hideyuki began to get up to see her to the door.

"You don't have to get up. Please, lie down."

"It's alright, never mind about me. Where are you planning to have the baby?"

She lent Hideyuki a hand as he braced himself against the wall and hobbled toward her. She mentioned the name of a local obstetrics clinic.

At that, Hideyuki stopped in his tracks.

"So you're not going to have it here."

She could sense reproach behind his words. The university hospital was close to his heart; he had lots of colleagues on the staff, and his son had studied there as a medical student. He no doubt felt that in an emergency, she'd get better care at the hospital than at some little clinic down the street.

Of course the idea had occurred to Reiko. But the fact that the hospital was where Ryoji had killed himself held her back.

"Well, I thought about it, but..."

Hideyuki couldn't know that her son had killed himself there. She hesitated to voice such inauspicious memories right now, so she was left floundering for a reason.

"You ought to have it here." Hideyuki was virtually pleading with her. He plainly wanted to see his grandchild as soon as he possibly could. He might have escaped a once-certain death, but he wouldn't be checking out of the hospital for quite some time yet. If she had the baby in the hospital, he could see it right away, and much more frequently after that.

Reiko understood all this, and it shook her. A mere thirty minutes of conversation had told her all she needed to know about Hideyuki. Even if he hadn't been Kaoru's father, she would have liked the man.

"I'll consider it."

In reply Hideyuki stretched out his hands to clasp hers. His hands felt like Kaoru's.

"Come back and visit again sometime. I'll be waiting."

Reiko had a feeling of déjà vu. Everything from the way he greeted her to the passionate grip of his hands was the way it had been with Kaoru. Only, now, the roles of visitor and visited were reversed.

As she closed the door behind her, she thought, *Maybe I should have the baby here after all.*

# 5

A month before she was due, Reiko began to slip back into melancholy. At night, alone in her room, her anxiety spiraled out of control, and she began to fear she was going mad. Winter was almost over. It was March now, nearly six months since Kaoru's departure.

Her condo was too big for someone living alone. With its huge living room and three bedrooms, it had been almost too much even when she'd lived there with her husband and son. Now its vastness oppressed her. It symbolized emptiness itself; she couldn't bear it. Having lost her loved ones one after the other, she was now alone—not strictly speaking, but close enough—in her fight. The enemy was no longer the MHC virus, but an overwhelming solitude.

The living room was crammed with luxurious furnishings, each one the product of her late entrepreneur husband's financial clout. They were without value now.

Reiko sank down onto the couch, pulled her knees up, and buried her face in them, sobbing. She couldn't figure out what to do to make up for the desolation she felt inside, a desolation so powerful it made her tremble. Her life was a bleak landscape stretching out before her. Though she told herself to live, despair was always with her.

*I just want someone to talk to.*

That was her sincerest wish. She was sure Hideyuki would play that role for her splendidly, if she wanted him to. They shared the same emotional wounds, and for that reason, among others, he was sure to be a good conversation partner. She'd already done the paperwork to specify the university hospital as the place where she was going to have the baby. But Hideyuki alone wouldn't be able to stave off her sudden attacks of loneliness—to help her master the enemy that occupied these rooms.

Reiko closed her eyes and tried to clear her mind of the spaciousness of the apartment. As she did so, a compact, edited version of her life played in her mind. A landscape made up of memorable events from her younger days—grade school, middle school, high school, college—floated before her mind's eye. An objectified view.

She knew exactly why she was seeing these third-party visions of her past. The other day, organizing her closets, she'd found, quite by accident, a floppy disc full of digital images.

They'd been assembled twelve years ago for display at her wedding. A rush of nostalgia came over her and she ended up looking through them again and again on the monitor. She'd provided the digital images herself, but her friends had edited them together into a light-hearted, even humorous version of her life. It had been ages since she'd looked at some of those pictures, and so, seeing what her friends had put together, she'd laughed out loud.

The sequence had been displayed on a huge screen in the wedding hall. It began with scenes of her as a baby and ended with a shot of her at twenty-two standing side-by-side with her future husband. It was hardly a complete picture, just a simple sketch of her life from ages zero to twenty-two.

Reiko paused on the last scene. It had been shot with a still camera, not a videocam; she and her future husband were standing with the ocean at their backs. Reiko wasn't facing the camera. Instead she was twisted to one side, sticking her belly out toward her husband. Why had she assumed such an awkward pose?

Reiko recalled the conversation they'd been having when the photo was taken. They weren't married yet, but already she was carrying her husband's child. She had wanted to make it clear in the photo that the child was being born because he was wanted, that he would enter life welcomed. That was why she'd stuck her belly out and placed her hand on it for the camera. She'd made no effort to hide her pregnancy from the wedding guests, either. The master of ceremonies had paused on the image and announced to the crowd that twenty-two-year-old Reiko was carrying the groom's child, and the two of them had been bathed in cheers.

When she closed her eyes she could hear the applause. She'd had everything back then. Her parents were still alive, the man who was to be her husband was at her side, and his child was growing within her. Ryoji.

She hung her head, helpless in the flood of memories. Reflecting on the past never assuaged her desolation but only made it worse. It wasn't good for her to be alone. As long as she was, her mind would always be under the sway of images from the past.

"That's it."

She got up from the sofa and went into the room with her AV equipment in it.

The room held a computer with a huge display. Amano had arranged it so that she could access and view the Loop from home.

She could access it: this didn't mean she could communicate with entities living within it. Simply watching them unilaterally could end up aggravating her frustration, but she decided not to let Amano's gesture go to waste. She followed his instructions and tried to call up an image from the Loop.

Amano must have preset it to focus on "Ryuji Takayama," because suddenly the monitor was filled with a close-up of Kaoru's face. Reiko cried out, remembering again how much she missed him.

Without any context, she didn't know where he was. Kaoru was lying on a couch, asleep. The couch looked like it might have been in the corner of a laboratory, but when she backed up her perspective-point, she realized it was actually a hospital waiting room.

In the Loop it was 1994. Three years had elapsed in it since the project's resumption. Having sacrificed himself and thereby contributed mightily to defeating the MHC virus in the real world, Kaoru had been reborn in the Loop as Ryuji Takayama to reverse cancerization there as well. He was thirty-seven now.

The youth of twenty Reiko had loved had now, in the space of six months, become a strong man three years older than her. The added years showed in his face, but they had given him a charm appropriate for his age. She could see that even when he was asleep. But he was in a hospital, waiting for his name to be called. She wondered if there was something wrong with him physically.

His name was called, and "Takayama" opened his eyes. He seemed to have momentarily forgotten where he was; it always happened when he dozed off. He glanced around him, and for a moment Reiko imagined that their gazes had met. Her chest tightened with joy. Unable to speak with him, she found herself interpreting each of his movements as they might relate to her, assigning some significance to everything.

Takayama went into an exam room and undressed to the waist, exposing his muscular body. Looking at him from behind, she could see a ten-centimeter scar running across his back. That hadn't been there when they were together. Had he gotten into an accident during his frantic activity in the Loop? The way the skin weltered up at the scar told her how serious the injury had been. Reiko got a funny feeling at the base of her spine from imagining him losing a lot of blood.

The examination took ten minutes. Takayama got

dressed and went out to the reception desk where he waited for a prescription to be issued. Behind him Reiko could see a dozen or so patients on the couches waiting for their appointments. One of them caught her eye, and she gasped. It was a young woman with delicately balanced features, sitting with her legs crossed. Everything about her face—from her prominent forehead to her straight eyebrows, from the undeviating line of her nose to the slightly cruel, thin lips—was perfect. But it wasn't her beauty that had made Reiko gasp. She'd seen that face before.

Reiko paused the image and zoomed in on the woman's face. It took her only a dozen or so seconds to recall the name.

*Sadako Yamamura.*

This was the woman who'd turned the Loop cancerous. She'd had the ability to record sounds on a tape reel without using a recorder, and she'd honed the ability to the point of making a lethal videotape. Her videotape had mutated, branching out into all sorts of media. When a woman who was ovulating came into contact with the images, she became pregnant with an entity that shared Sadako's DNA. Reiko vividly recalled watching Sadako crawl out of the womb of that woman who'd fallen into the rooftop exhaust shaft—the newborn, gnawing through the umbilical cord with toothless gums. Pregnant herself, Reiko had been unable to see it as merely virtual, as something totally unrelated to her. Though it had taken place in an entirely different space, in the Loop, just watching it she'd shivered with horror.

That was how the Loop world had been unmoored in a flood of mutated media, all reproducing a single DNA pattern with astonishing speed.

And now the culprit, Sadako Yamamura herself, was sitting right behind Takayama, waiting for her exam with a look of total innocence on her face. Once he'd received his prescription, Takayama seemed to notice her, but his expression didn't change. He walked out of the hospital. It looked to be just an ordinary, everyday event.

In the hospital lobby Takayama passed another Sadako Yamamura. They both just kept walking, in opposite directions, hardly noticing each other. Takayama went into the parking lot outside the hospital entrance and opened the door to his car, while Sadako got onto an elevator inside the hospital and went up to a higher floor.

Takayama started his car. Reiko didn't know where he was heading, but he drove onto a trunk road and then stepped on the accelerator. Scenery started rushing past at high speed...

Reiko lost track of time as she watched. No longer was she able to see this as a television show, unrelated to her. She was watching a person's life. The images conveyed the uninvented truth about an irreplaceable man.

## 6

Every day for the next month, at a predetermined time, Reiko accessed the Loop and peeked in on Takayama's life. It could be said without exaggeration that this was the only joy she was getting out of life. Since time in the Loop moved at six times the rate it did in the real world, when she accessed it at the appointed time every day, she was watching images six days newer than the previous day's. She was only getting fragments, a few hours out of every six days, but it was more manageable that way. It would have been a waste of time to follow a life in its entirety. Better to take fragments and fill in the gaps with her imagination.

And by doing so she was able to understand the general unfolding of events. She watched sequences having to do with halting the cancerization of the Loop and recovering its biodiversity—events in which Takayama played a big part. Watching them gave her so much joy that she wanted to shout out loud.

She became more and more engrossed in watching the progress of the Loop world. As the Loop recovered, the loneliness weighing on Reiko started to disperse: the two processes began to resonate with each other, settling into a common rhythm. Takayama's actions were directly lifting Reiko's heart.

The Loop had literally begun to die, once. Once the denizens of the Loop had learned about the killer video-tape and the mutated manifestations of it in other media, panic had set in, a panic that had the ironic effect of accelerating the spread of the virus. People didn't wait for the end of their week's grace period, and they weren't satisfied with showing the tape to just one other person. Some individuals showed it to a host of other people. Reiko was able to experience several variations on the process: people killing each other because of the tape, love affairs falling apart, people scheming to save loved ones. It was like watching a detailed picture of hell, with egotism on full display in all its forms. It was like watching the real world.

The world looked like it was going to end, but that wasn't how things went, thanks to the coming of Takayama to the Loop world.

Takayama did two things to prevent the canceriza-tion of the Loop world. Three months ago, when Reiko had met him in Amano's laboratory, he had already suc-ceeded in synthesizing a vaccine. That was no doubt one reason he could say "It's going to be alright" with such confidence. Since then, the vaccine had begun to prove itself effective.

Individuals who had come into contact with the mutated manifestations of the tape were programmed to die in a week or to become impregnated with the ring virus. It was simply a question of how to disable that program. Takayama approached the problem that way, according to the hypothesis formulated in the world in which he'd existed as Kaoru, and succeeded in developing the necessary technology. It wasn't all that difficult a task for him because he thoroughly knew how the world worked. The vaccine did two things for those inoculated with it: it disabled the program, and it gave people resistance to the program being installed again.

As the vaccine came to be manufactured in quantity and more and more people were inoculated, the mutated forms of the tape came to pose less of a threat. Instead of a deadly weapon they were now simply junk. They were allowed to fulfill their purpose as entertainment, but that was all anyone saw them as.

*People used to call this the Killer Video. Are you brave enough to watch it?*

It was becoming a relic of the past.

But there was another problem: what to do about all the Sadako Yamamuras who had flooded the world. The Sadakos were hermaphroditic, and they could reproduce on their own, so it was still possible for them to multiply with viral speed. The media terror may have died out, but if the Sadakos continued to occupy a larger and larger percentage of the human population, the Loop ecology was still in danger. Otherwise the Sadakos were harmless, and public opinion wasn't hysteric enough, or the public will wasn't firm enough, to eliminate them. Some said this was the logical stance, but it was probably more accurate to say that everyone recoiled from the question of who was going to hunt down the Sadakos and dispose of them, and how.

However, a new virus was unleashed that resolved things perfectly. It was unclear whether it had existed in the Loop world all along and had simply mutated into a state of efficacy or if it had been intentionally designed, but either way, it inflicted decisive damage on the Sadakos and no one else. Left to its natural course, it effectively destroyed the source of all the problems. And in the process, the events left a warning for society as a whole, an eloquent testament to the risks of losing diversity and allowing all life to become assimilated to one pattern.

An organic community's resilience is directly tied to the presence of individual differences within it. Some live in the mountains, some live by the sea. Some live in a world of ice, some under equatorial conditions. Some have white skin, some black. The greater the range of individual differences, the greater the chances of surviving a catastrophic blow. A virus can harm individual beings that live in hot places while having no effect on ones that live in cold places. If it attacked both, the former would die while the latter would survive. As long as there are survivors, there can always be a new start—a chance to form a world with sufficient diversity. But if the entire world shares the same DNA, everyone in it runs the risk of succumbing to the same viral attack.

The virus that overcame the Sadakos served as proof of that. It seemed to work upon some physical peculiar-

# BIRTHDAY

ity of the Sadakos, which caused them to die a natural death.

The Sadakos were not born through sexual reproduction, and they shared the characteristic of growing to maturity in a week's time. Once they contracted the virus, however, they grew old at the same advanced rate until they died of natural causes. The Loop world began to overflow with aging, dying Sadakos.

Reiko found herself curiously moved by the sight of Sadakos dying in the streets. She knew how much the original Sadako had dreaded getting old in her days as an actress—as a woman, Reiko couldn't bear to see her succumbing helplessly to the hideousness of age. The fact that it wasn't just one Sadako but myriads who were fighting and losing the battle only made it sadder.

The Loop world seemed to believe that the virus that was killing the Sadakos had arisen naturally. Reiko suspected that it was man-made, and she thought she knew by whom. Ryuji Takayama—Kaoru. She believed that he had taken his knowledge of the unique telomerase sequence in his own DNA and applied it to creating a virus that hastened cellular division. Amano had told her about the correlation between aging and the number of times a cell divided, and how the latter was limited by the length of the telomeres.

So, in the end, Takayama had created two products: a vaccine to disable the program that brought death or impregnation, and a virus to increase the rate of the clones' cellular division. Together these allowed the

Loop world to recover its biodiversity.

Reiko moved her perspective-point back to widen her field of vision. In hundred meter increments, she gradually rose to a vantage point of several kilometers over the surface of the Loop world. Finally leaving the atmosphere, she noticed that the ball known as the Loop had changed color ever so slightly. It was beautiful now, hardly different from Earth.

Until a short time ago it had been covered here and there with dirty splotches, but now, with its biodiversity restored, the Loop world was returning to its original color. This was a mixture of many different hues, reflected in delicate shades, darkness and brightness added according to the light.

Reiko was relieved to see this. It was visual confirmation that Kaoru had accomplished the mission he'd gone down into the Loop to perform. The beauty and brightness of the image told her this faster than any words could have.

She wanted to go to sleep clinging to this feeling of relief.

She turned off the computer, thinking she'd watch more tomorrow, and lay her pregnant body down on the bed. She could feel the fetus kicking energetically inside her. It could come at any time now. She pulled the telephone up next to her pillow, just in case.

The next day, at the same time, Reiko accessed the Loop again. Six days had passed in the Loop world, and in just that short time, a change had come over Takayama's body. He was in the hospital again. He was in the same exam room, and he was undressing in front of the doctor again.

Reiko was looking at his back. In addition to the scar slanting across his back, she could see brown spots on his skin, and wrinkles on his neck. The change was drastic for such a short period of time. His hair was going white, and his hands, as he picked up his clothing, were dry and cracked.

Reiko took her vantage point around to the front and looked at his face. What she hadn't dared think before became a certainty now. The face she was looking at had changed. It was old.

It was Takayama, no doubt of that. His belly and chest still looked youthful. The contrast between them and his aged face put Reiko in mind of some unnatural power. Her anxiety grew.

The exam over, Takayama went to the reception desk for his prescription and then tottered out of the hospital. As he did, Reiko's monitor showed her the waiting room, where she'd previously seen two Sadakos in a brief moment; now there were none. Had they been completely expelled from the Loop world?

Takayama left the building and walked down the street. This time he wasn't driving, but walking along the pavement.

His shrunken back bore witness to extreme fatigue and physical decline. Walking seemed difficult for him.

Every now and then he'd stop and lean against an electrical pole or a wall, press on his chest and wheeze and cough.

Each time, he'd take out the medicine he'd just been prescribed and swallow a little, but he himself seemed to realize it was good for nothing but psychological comfort.

Obviously, Takayama was overcome by rapid aging. Reiko thought she could guess why. He'd become infected with the same virus that had aged the Sadakos. He must have foreseen it when he was developing the virus. Given the similarities of their manner of resurrection into the Loop world, the virus was bound to affect him as well, to kill him. He'd known it but gone through with it anyway. He'd sacrificed himself twice over. He was a man burdened by fate.

When he could no longer stand, he made his way between some buildings to a set of steps leading up into a park and sat down on them. She could imagine him feeling the coolness of the concrete beneath him. What season was it, she wondered. Passersby looked to be dressed for chilly weather.

Sitting there on the concrete steps, Takayama was surrounded by people but steeped in a stunning solitude. Nobody knew him as their messiah; everybody simply walked by without noticing him. Reiko was seized with a desire to reach out and touch his body so they could tend to each other's loneliness. If only she could. She was so close, but she couldn't even really hold his hand. For the first time since she'd begun accessing the Loop, she felt violently annoyed at the setup.

Takayama was leaning forward, hands resting on his weakly splayed knees. Sometimes he would lift his head and gaze at the sky; when he did, he looked strangely refreshed. Did he feel like he'd lived out his allotment of days? He'd certainly been through his share of death and rebirth. He looked like a man who had composed himself to meet a natural death, secure in the satisfaction of having accomplished his task. He stretched out his bent frame and leaned back against the steps. He looked more comfortable than before.

He was almost supine now, and she had a good view of the expression on his face. He was looking straight in her direction. He could probably see the sky from that space between tall buildings. But his stare seemed ready to penetrate to Reiko's side of the monitor.

Takayama started to say something to the sky but closed his mouth and licked his dry lips.

*What's he trying to say?*

His mouth opened only to clamp shut again several times.

Remembering Amano's instructions, Reiko tapped out some commands on the keyboard and locked into Takayama's perspective. It would allow her to see with her own eyes what Takayama was seeing with his.

The scenery changed, and just as she'd expected, the monitor showed her a small patch of blue sky between the tops of buildings. Reiko was now looking at the world through Takayama's eyes. It moved her to think that she was seeing the way he was seeing. When she looked more closely, she saw something resembling a human face floating in the sky.

Reiko recognized the face. She saw it in the mirror every day: it was her.

*He's thinking of me right now and imagining my face.*

Reiko felt Kaoru's feelings with painful intensity. Even after he closed his eyes, the image of her face hovered there against the backs of his eyelids. She could actually see the strength of Kaoru's thoughts. He wanted her so much that his mind was creating her face for him. Reiko could see it with her own eyes.

Only when the face in the sky started to blur and become double did Reiko become aware of her tears. With Takayama's heart in her breast, she tried to imagine what it was he'd been trying to say—or not to say.

It seemed to her that, on the verge of death, he was reflecting on how happy he'd been with her. That made Reiko far happier than hearing him say goodbye.

The beating of his heart grew slower and fainter. Death was approaching. The scene wobbled slightly. He seemed to be having a hard time keeping his head up.

Now his eyes stayed closed for longer stretches than they were open. At length, his surroundings faded away. The skyscrapers, the trees, the crowds of people, all disappeared, and his field of vision was swathed in darkness. Reiko's face alone remained distinct. It stayed that way for a long time among the echoes of death.

The Loop world meant nothing to Reiko now. Seeing Takayama's final visions through the monitor made a far deeper impression on her than simply hearing about his death ever could. She disengaged from his point of view and allowed herself to stare at the Loop world from above for a time, lost. She knew that she had to accept Takayama's death calmly, just as he himself had. But she couldn't, not yet.

Later, when she'd managed to get herself somewhat under control, she eased her gaze away from the monitor. Her interest in the Loop world had faded now that Takayama was no longer in it.

*Goodbye.*

She turned off the power so that the virtual world disappeared from before her eyes. She would probably never look into it again.

It had only been for an instant, but Reiko had experienced death vicariously; strangely, she'd done so while seeing her own face through the eyes of someone she loved.

She didn't know if that was the reason, but a change had come over her body. Her labor pains hadn't exactly started yet, but her intuition was telling her:

*It's coming.*

She reached for the phone and dialed the number she'd been given.

# 7

Labor pains belonging to the first stage of childbirth came and went with a gentle rhythm. The fetus, which had been moving about so actively, quieted a bit now and moved to a lower position. Reiko felt as if a buoyant void occupied her chest area.

She climbed into a taxi and gave the name of the hospital.

"Having a baby?" the driver asked, and gently eased the car forward.

A large travel bag rested in her lap. She'd packed it some time ago with the things she'd need for the stay. When Ryoji was born she hadn't needed to make any preparations. Her mother and husband had sat on either side of her in the car, holding her hands and encouraging her to "hang in there." Now she was on her own, and nervous.

She arrived at the hospital at exactly seven o'clock pm. She changed clothes and lay down on a bed to wait for her cervix to dilate completely.

The labor pains made her think of massive undulations. The intervals were shorter than the rising and falling of the tide, but somewhat longer than those between waves crashing onto a beach. Grimacing with pain, Reiko called Kaoru's name. It seemed like it might distract her from the pain to talk to Kaoru—he would be beside her, watching over her.

In between the waves, Reiko's ears picked up music. At first she thought it was a radio in a neighboring room, but that didn't seem right.

She looked at the window, at the darkness it framed, and realized that the birth was going to last far into the night. She couldn't imagine that the music was coming from beyond the darkness. Maybe the hospital was playing some kind of background music for the fetus's benefit.

The music was soft, the melody mysterious and beautiful; it briefly lessened Reiko's suffering.

All at once she placed the source of the music. She could hardly believe it as she raised her head and stared at her belly.

"Stop singing down there and come out already."

She fantasized about her own son singing in the dark womb to ease his mother's suffering. Maybe the events of the Loop were still with her; she was starting to confuse the relationship between protector and protected, container and contained.

By a little after eleven, her cervix had completely dilated. Reiko was taken from the labor room to the delivery room and placed on the delivery table.

She started pushing in time with her labor pains, following the instructions of the doctor and the nurse. The rhythm was quicker now than before, and the contractions of her uterus and abdominal muscles kept pace.

She could feel all the strength in her body concentrating in an effort to push the baby out.

She tried to switch to abdominal breathing like the nurse told her to, but it was difficult. Between the pain and her nervousness, the deep belly breaths she tried to take ended up as quick shallow ones. She needed to relax. She thought of Kaoru's face again and began to talk to him.

"Don't speak!"

She was calling Kaoru's name now with every groan, every ragged breath that escaped from the corners of her mouth. Each time, the nurse cautioned her not to talk— it was wasting energy that she needed for the delivery.

Then the nurse gave a little cry and looked at the doctor. It had looked, just for a moment, like the baby's head had peeked out from Reiko's vagina.

The doctor gave a long sigh beneath his mask and clicked his tongue. He looked worried.

"She was dilated when she was brought in here, wasn't she?"

It wasn't really a question aimed at the nurse. He was just muttering to himself, confirming what he already knew. Her cervix, which had been dilated up until a few moments ago, had closed again.

Reiko had sensed something in their conversation, in the atmosphere of the room. She raised her head. "What's wrong?"

"Oh, nothing."

The doctor had no choice but to give a vague answer, not wanting her to worry. But Reiko showed no hesitation about putting into words what the doctor was beginning to fear.

"Did my baby go back inside?"

"Well, that's certainly what it looks like." There was something so childlike about the way Reiko had spoken, it did away with the doctor's apprehensions and put him in a slightly mirthful mood. "Why don't we just wait a little while?"

Mother and fetus were both doing just fine, and it looked like there would be no harm in letting nature take its course. The energy involved in birth all went in one direction; there was no chance it was going to reverse itself. They took Reiko back to the labor room, where she settled down to wait for a while longer.

If the labor pains of a few moments ago had been a raging storm, Reiko now felt like she was in the middle of an evening calm. The waves had been immense—where had they gone? Now that she asked herself that, Reiko began to find the peaceful respite unnerving. She could recall the exact instant when the energy shifted gently. When the nurse had given her little cry, Reiko had immediately known what it meant—she'd been about to cry out herself. She'd felt the air move against her skin right then.

"Hurry up and come out."

Somehow it seemed like the baby was reluctant, as if, having gotten a glimpse of the outside world, it was trying to decide if it was a place worth going out into.

Reiko looked at the white wall beyond her distended tummy and addressed her child.

"It's a pretty good place out here, you know."

She placed her hands on her abdomen and checked for movement, but there was no reply.

She glanced at the clock beside her pillow and closed her eyes. It was almost one in the morning. It had only been six hours since she'd checked in. She tried to calm down, telling herself it was still early.

An hour later the nurse came back to check on her. Nothing much had changed. "Hang in there," she said, and left.

Right after that, Reiko had a mighty contraction. It felt like the entire contents of her abdomen were going to be pushed out. She groped for the buzzer beside her pillow but couldn't find it.

*The baby's coming!*

As that maternal intuition coursed through her body, consciousness receded.

The next day Reiko was lying in bed with a peaceful look on her face as the preceding night's struggle receded to the far side of memory, to be replaced by a drowsy, languid satisfaction. The pain of delivery had been transformed into the moving feeling of having delivered; joy welled up from deep within her.

A baby cried, right next to her. It wasn't in bed with her. The nurse was dandling it in her arms.

Reiko observed the baby's expression almost unconsciously. It was a boy, just as expected. Something about his face made him look like his father.

Behind the nurse was a thick pane of glass separating the nursery from the outside to keep it germ-free. The glass also acted like a mirror, reflecting the nurse and the baby. The real scene and the fictive one in the glass faced each other and swayed in the same direction.

Reiko could see the hint of a tall form looking down at the baby reflected in the glass. It was just a hint, a shade. It leaned over and brought its face close to the baby's, gazing at it, as if to whisper something to it.

The outlines of the image became clearer, its features more defined.

*Kaoru.*

Reiko raised her head, faced the image, and called to it. She had the feeling that words he'd tried to speak but couldn't before were finally emerging from his mouth.

*Happy birthday.*

The words tumbled from his lips, celebrating, not a day, but birth itself.

Reiko thought with pleasure: when her son grew older, how she'd tell him about his father, and watch his exploits together. This vision of the future made her heart dance. She was sure her son would be proud of the man his father'd been.

Reiko cradled Kaoru's words and repeated them to their son.

*Happy birthday.*

## ABOUT THE AUTHOR

Koji Suzuki was born in 1957 in Hamamatsu, southwest of Tokyo. He attended Keio University where he majored in French. After graduating he held numerous odd jobs, including a stint as a cram school teacher. Also a self-described jock, he holds a first-class yachting license and crossed the U.S., from Key West to Los Angeles, on his motorcycle.

The father of two daughters, Suzuki is a respected authority on childrearing and has written numerous works on the subject. He acquired his expertise when he was a struggling writer and househusband. Suzuki also has translated a children's book into Japanese, *The Little Sod Diaries* by the crime novelist Simon Brett.

In 1990, Suzuki's first full-length work, *Paradise*, won the Japanese Fantasy Novel Award and launched his career as a fiction writer. *Ring*, written with a baby on his lap, catapulted him to fame, and the multi-million selling sequels *Spiral* and *Loop* cemented his reputation as a world-class talent. Often called the "Stephen King of Japan," Suzuki has played a crucial role in establishing mainstream credentials for horror novels in his country. He is based in Tokyo but loves to travel, often in the United States. *Birthday* is his sixth work to appear in English.

# First it was a videotape. Then it was a virus. Now it is a universe.

The Ring trilogy
complete
in paperback

RING

SPIRAL

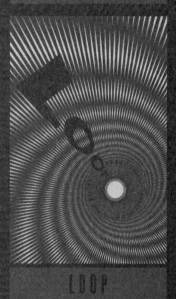

LOOP

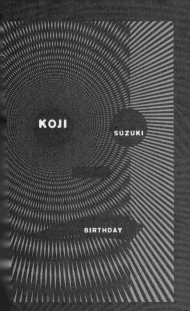

# BIRTHDAY

This much-awaited return to the *Ring* universe features three short stories focusing on its female characters, with a theme of birth. An exploration of extraordinary circumstances from the perspectives of memorable women, *Birthday* is no mere sequel—as fans of *Spiral* and *Loop* should know.

## Sequels to the *Ring* Trilogy

### AVAILABLE NOW!

# S

Takanori Ando, son of *Spiral* protagonist Mitsuo, works at a small CGI production company and hopes to become a filmmaker one day despite coming from a family of doctors. When he's tasked by his boss to examine a putatively streamed video of a suicide that's been floating around the internet, the aspiring director takes on more than he bargained for.

# EDGE

When a team of scientists tests new computer hardware by calculating the value of pi into the deep decimals, the figures begin to repeat a pattern. It's mathematically untenable – unless the physical constants that undergird our universe have altered, ever so slightly... *Winner of the Shirley Jackson Award.*

## PARADISE

In the arid badlands of prehistoric Asia, a lovelorn youth violates a sacred tribal taboo against representing human figures by etching an image of his beloved. When the foretold punishment comes to pass, the two must embark on a journey across the world, and time itself, to try to reclaim their destiny. A mysterious spirit guides them towards a surprise destination that readers may indeed find quite close to home.

## DARK WATER

haunting collection of short stories om Koji Suzuki, author of the smash riller, *Ring*, which spawned the hit m and sequels. The first story in this llection has been adapted to film *ark Water*, Walter Salles), and another, drift" is currently in production as a rren Aronofsky film.

# NOW!

## Basis of the blockbuster PlayStation games Parasite Eve 1&2

"Sena's work in pharmacology and microbiology lends th Japanese import a sense of discovery and fear that resonat when new science is not fully understood. SF and horror fa who liked Koji Suzuki's *Ring*...will find *Parasite Eve* a chilli tale on a cellular level; recommended." —*Library Journal*

"*Parasite Eve* combines Michael Crichton's scientific cutti edge plausibility with David Cronenberg's abject flesh/sex h ror. Throw in *Frankenstein* and *The Blob*, synthesize, a enjoy." —*Fangoria* magazine

Eve is a parasitic mitochondria reproducing itself at alarm speed. Her goal? To take over mankind.

### Parasite Eve
by Hideaki Sena
1-932234-19-5
$24.95/$31.95, 320 pages
Hardcover

# Vertical Horror
## beyond the *Ring* series

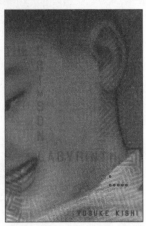

### *LOST* meets *Battle Royale*

"Making a survival game in the desert is in and of itsel ple, but the meta-game issues behind the motives of s game's creation makes for a great twist in the p it...Yusuke Kishi's strength as a storyteller is unshakab *Ronza magazine*

"*The Crimson Labyrinth* starts out like a game, with its ified build-up of knowledge and description of survival how, dangerous drugs, poisonous snakes. Once you reading this book, you won't be able to put it down." —*Lee* magazine

Nine unemployed men and women show up for a job in and wake up in the Australian outback. They've been d by a media crew that may or may not be the real puppet in this psycho-horror knockout. *The Crimson Labyrinth* w you questioning every turn in the suspense.

### The Crimson Labyrinth
by Yusuke Kishi
1-932234-11-X
$14.95/$21.00, 288 pages
Paperback